THE HUNGER
OF THE
SEVEN SQUAT BEARS

ÉMILE BRAVO

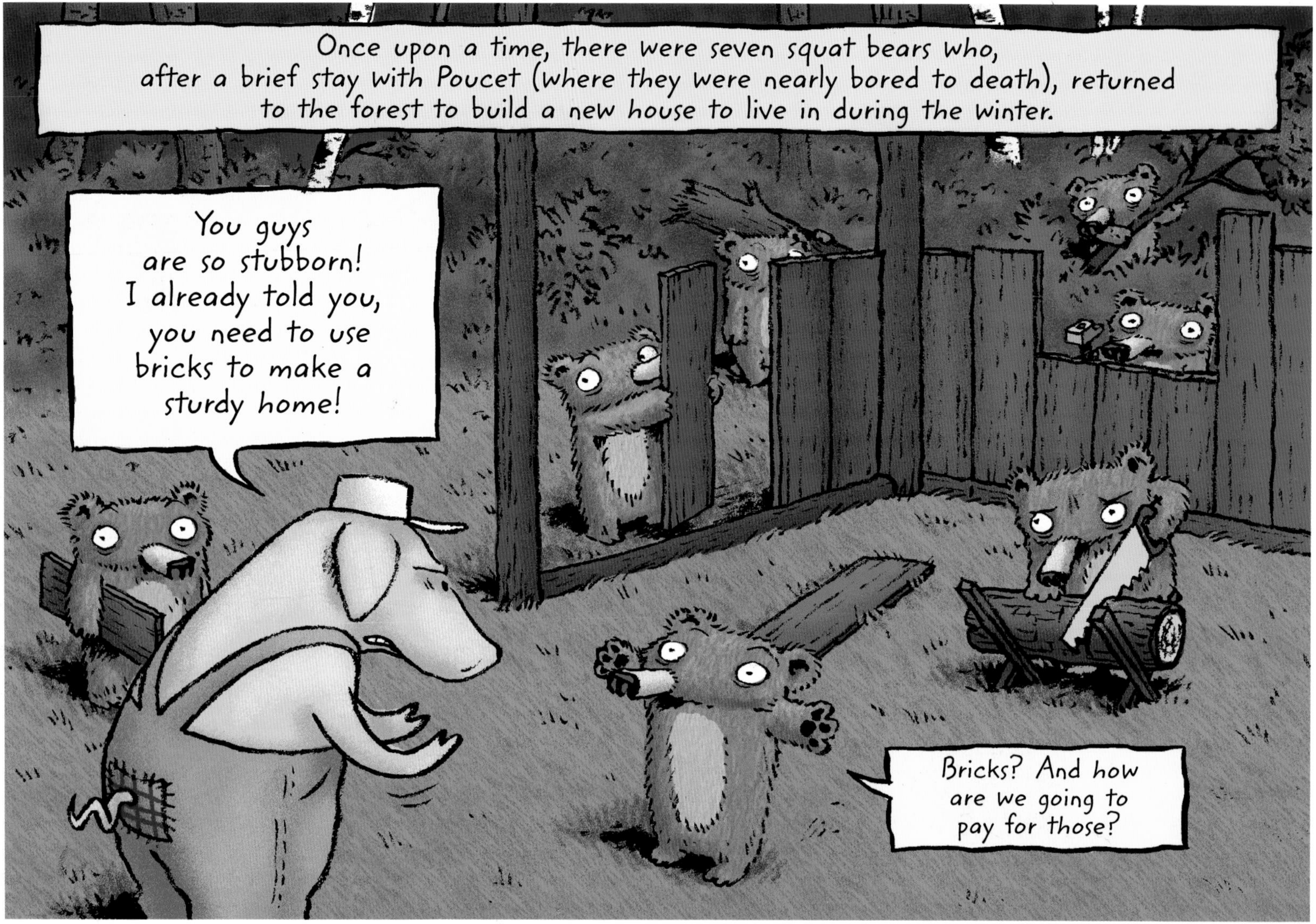
Once upon a time, there were seven squat bears who, after a brief stay with Poucet (where they were nearly bored to death), returned to the forest to build a new house to live in during the winter.
You guys are so stubborn! I already told you, you need to use bricks to make a sturdy home!
Bricks? And how are we going to pay for those?

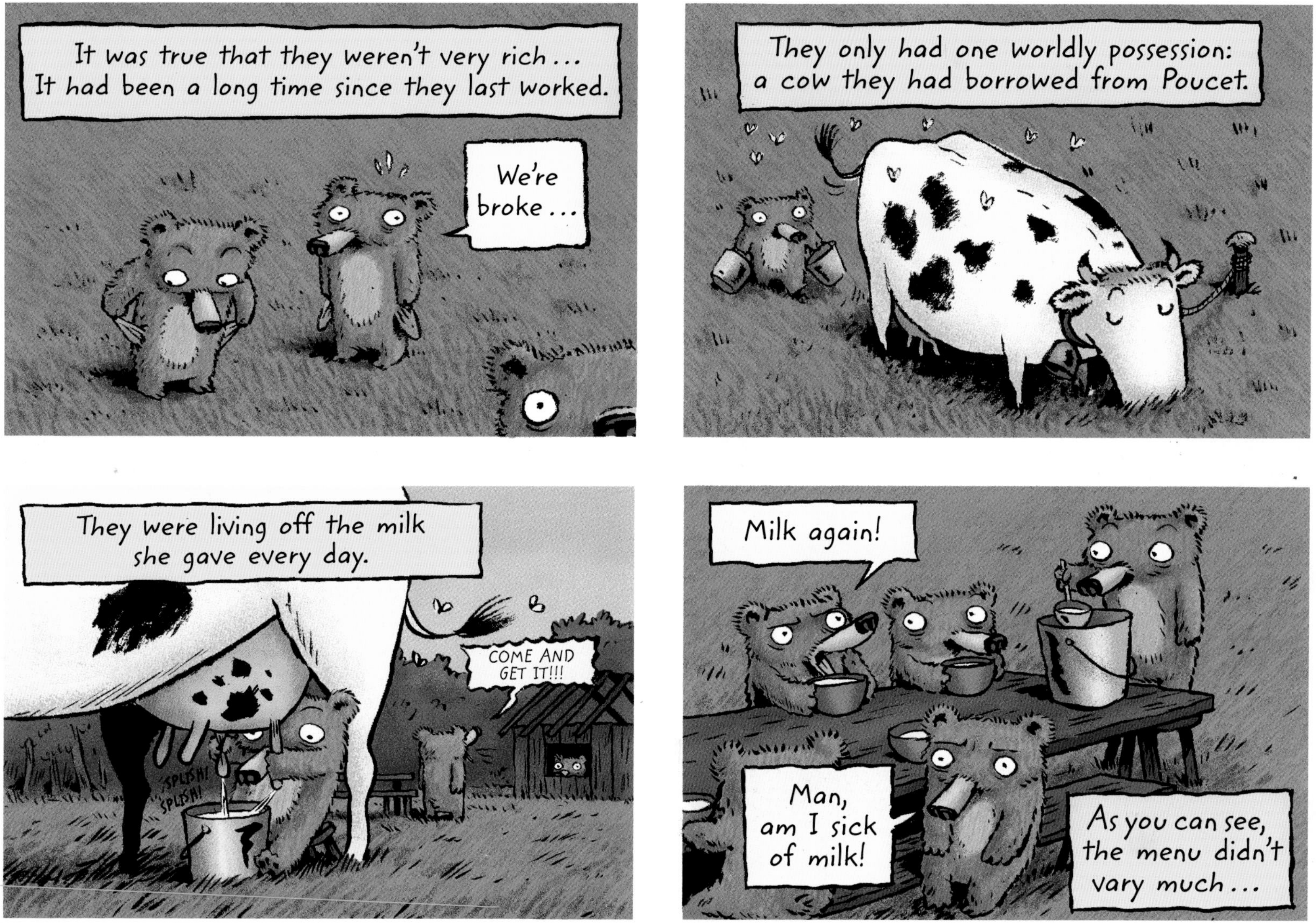
It was true that they weren't very rich... It had been a long time since they last worked.
We're broke...
They only had one worldly possession: a cow they had borrowed from Poucet.
They were living off the milk she gave every day.
SPLISH! SPLISH!
COME AND GET IT!!!
Milk again!
Man, am I sick of milk!
As you can see, the menu didn't vary much...

One day, one of the bears was so fed up with milk that he came up with an idea.

You! Go down to the market and sell the cow. Get a good price, and use the money to buy some butter. That would be a nice change from the milk.

Why me?

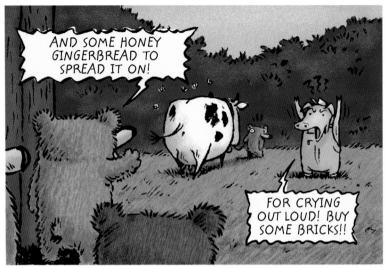

AND SOME HONEY GINGERBREAD TO SPREAD IT ON!

FOR CRYING OUT LOUD! BUY SOME BRICKS!!

Honey gingerbread is made with honey... Bears adore it.

Oh yeah! I'd give anything for a piece of bread...

Yeah, they definitely like honey...

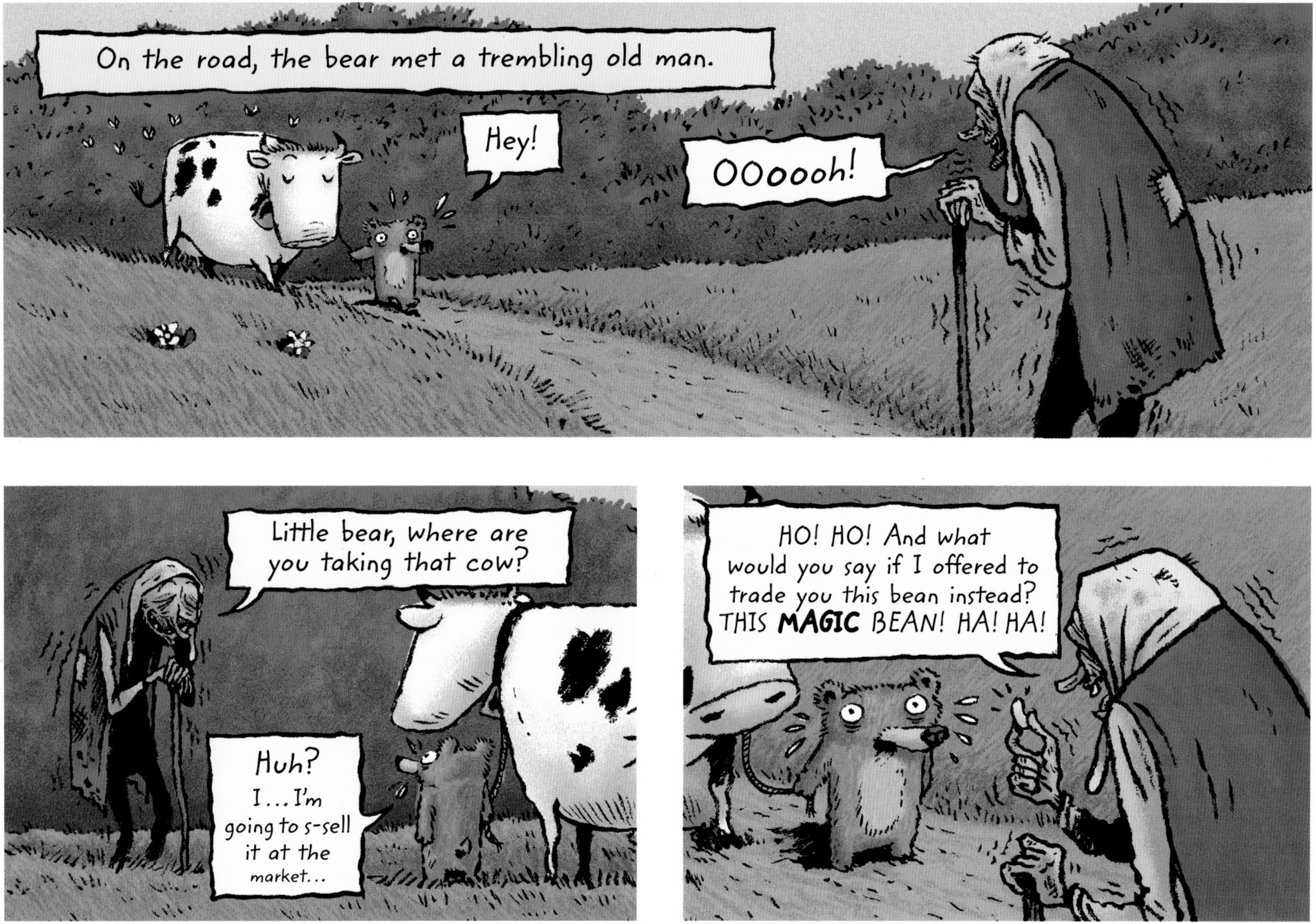
On the road, the bear met a trembling old man.
Hey!
OOoooh!
Little bear, where are you taking that cow?
Huh? I... I'm going to s-sell it at the market...
HO! HO! And what would you say if I offered to trade you this bean instead? THIS **MAGIC** BEAN! HA! HA!

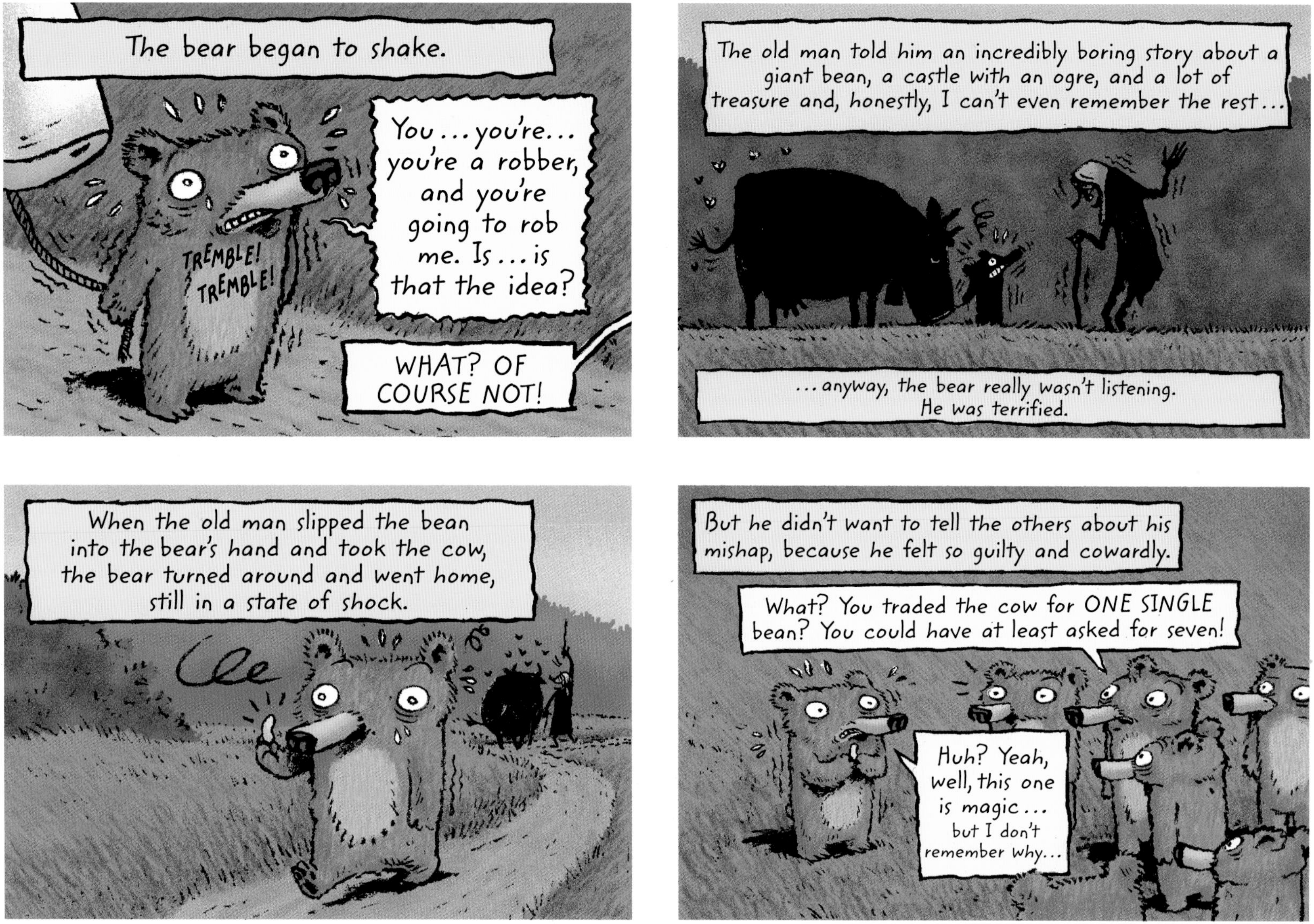
The bear began to shake.
You... you're... you're a robber, and you're going to rob me. Is... is that the idea?
TREMBLE! TREMBLE!
WHAT? OF COURSE NOT!
The old man told him an incredibly boring story about a giant bean, a castle with an ogre, and a lot of treasure and, honestly, I can't even remember the rest...
...anyway, the bear really wasn't listening. He was terrified.
When the old man slipped the bean into the bear's hand and took the cow, the bear turned around and went home, still in a state of shock.
But he didn't want to tell the others about his mishap, because he felt so guilty and cowardly.
What? You traded the cow for ONE SINGLE bean? You could have at least asked for seven!
Huh? Yeah, well, this one is magic... but I don't remember why...

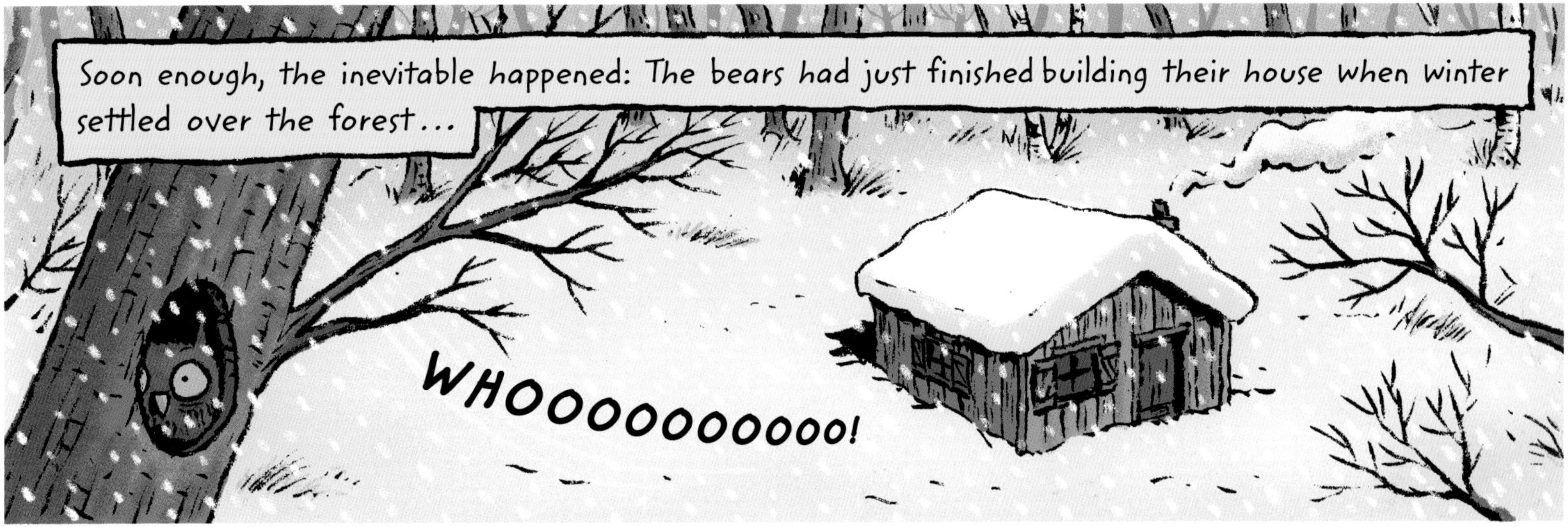
Soon enough, the inevitable happened: The bears had just finished building their house when winter settled over the forest...
WHOOOOOOOOOOO!

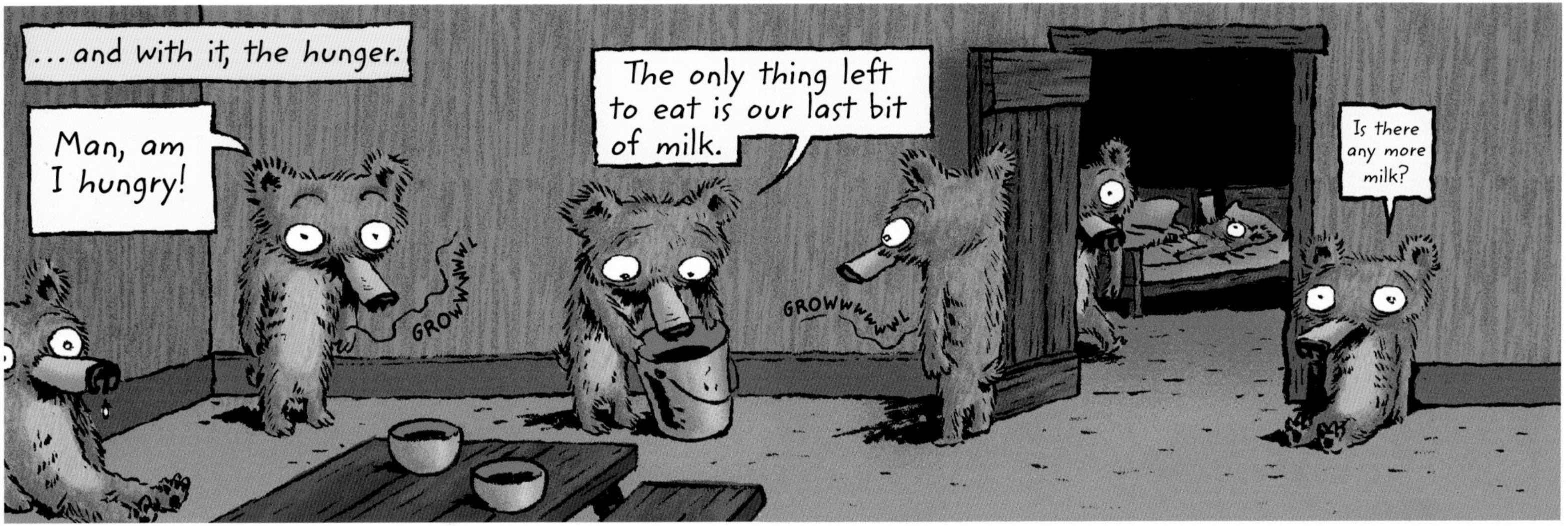
...and with it, the hunger.
Man, am I hungry!
GROWWWWWL
The only thing left to eat is our last bit of milk.
GROWWWWWWL
Is there any more milk?

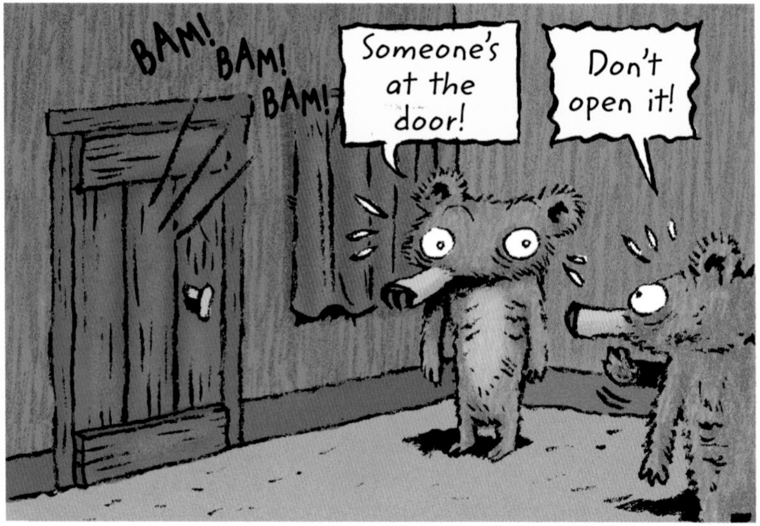
BAM! BAM! BAM!
Someone's at the door!
Don't open it!

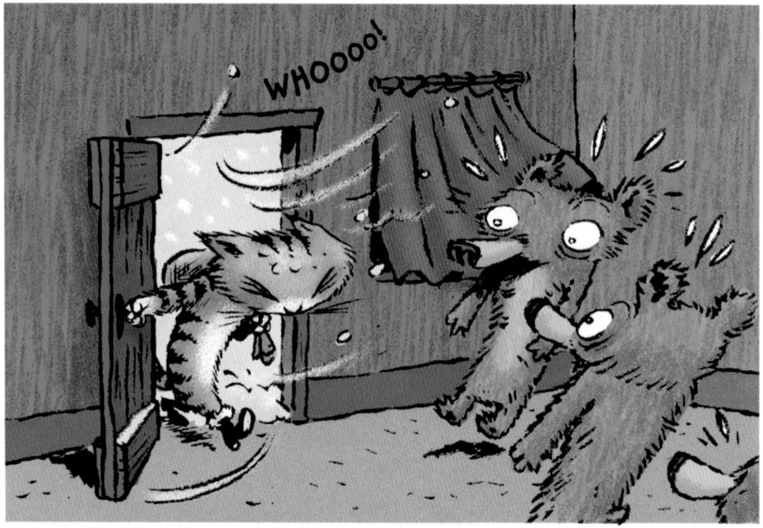
WHOOOO!

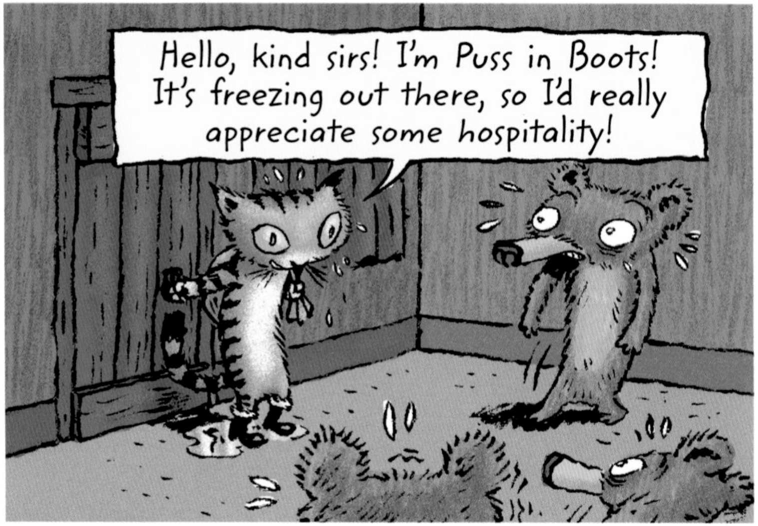
Hello, kind sirs! I'm Puss in Boots! It's freezing out there, so I'd really appreciate some hospitality!

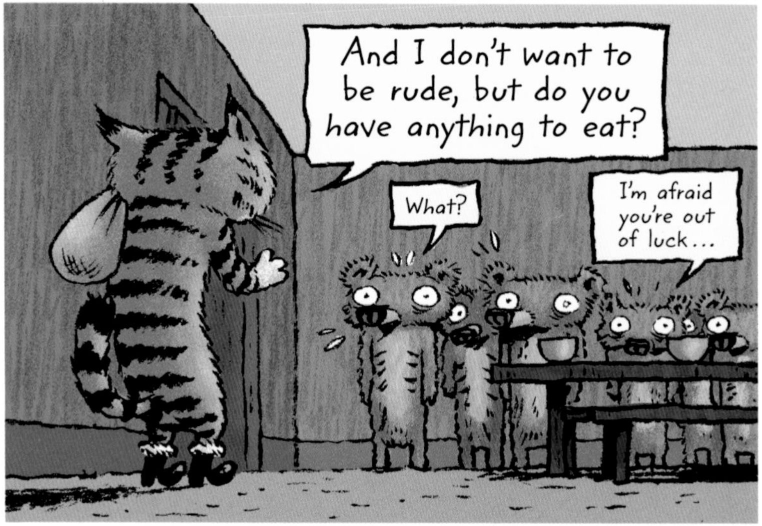
And I don't want to be rude, but do you have anything to eat?
What?
I'm afraid you're out of luck...

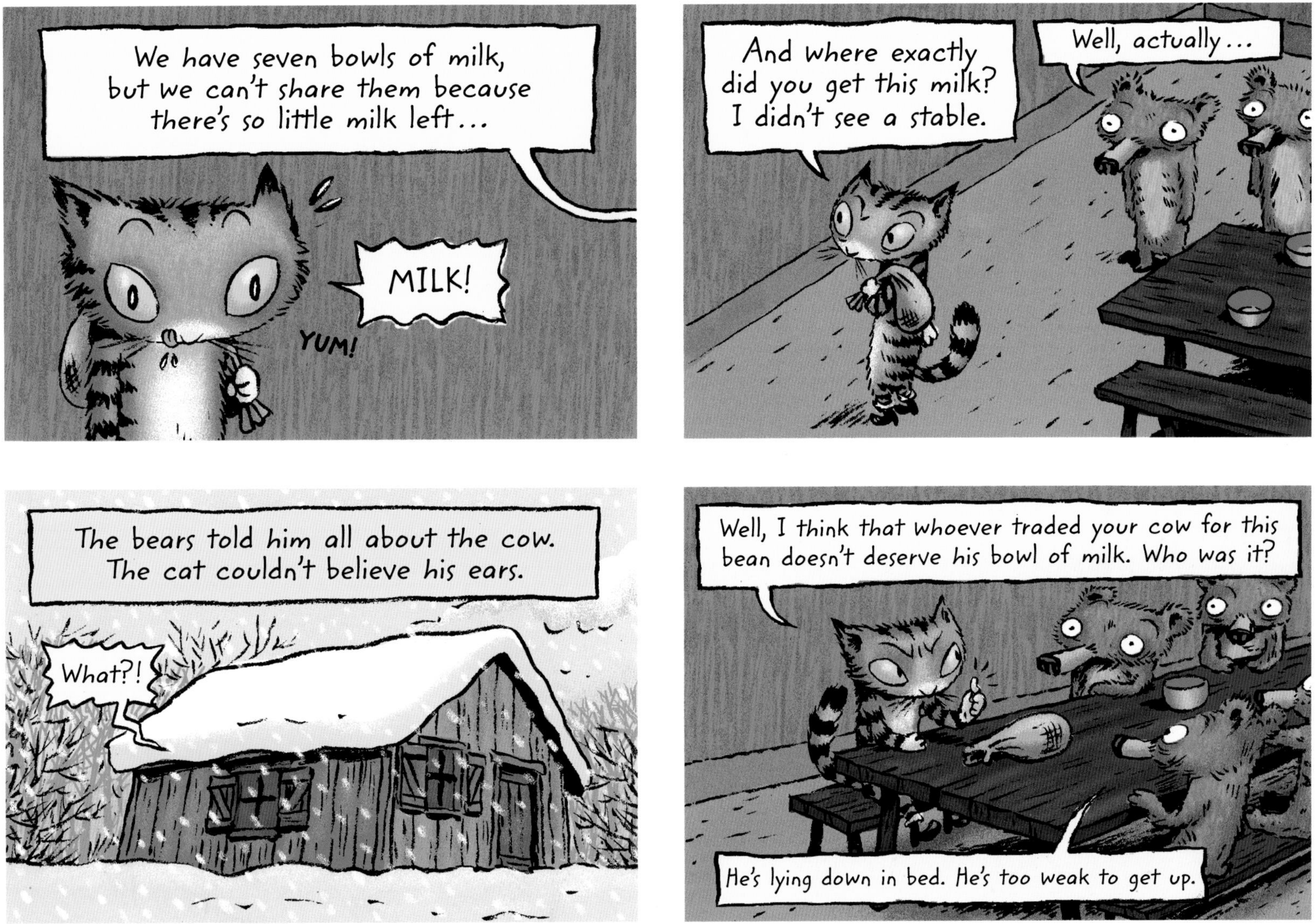
We have seven bowls of milk, but we can't share them because there's so little milk left...
MILK!
YUM!
And where exactly did you get this milk? I didn't see a stable.
Well, actually...
The bears told him all about the cow. The cat couldn't believe his ears.
What?!
Well, I think that whoever traded your cow for this bean doesn't deserve his bowl of milk. Who was it?
He's lying down in bed. He's too weak to get up.

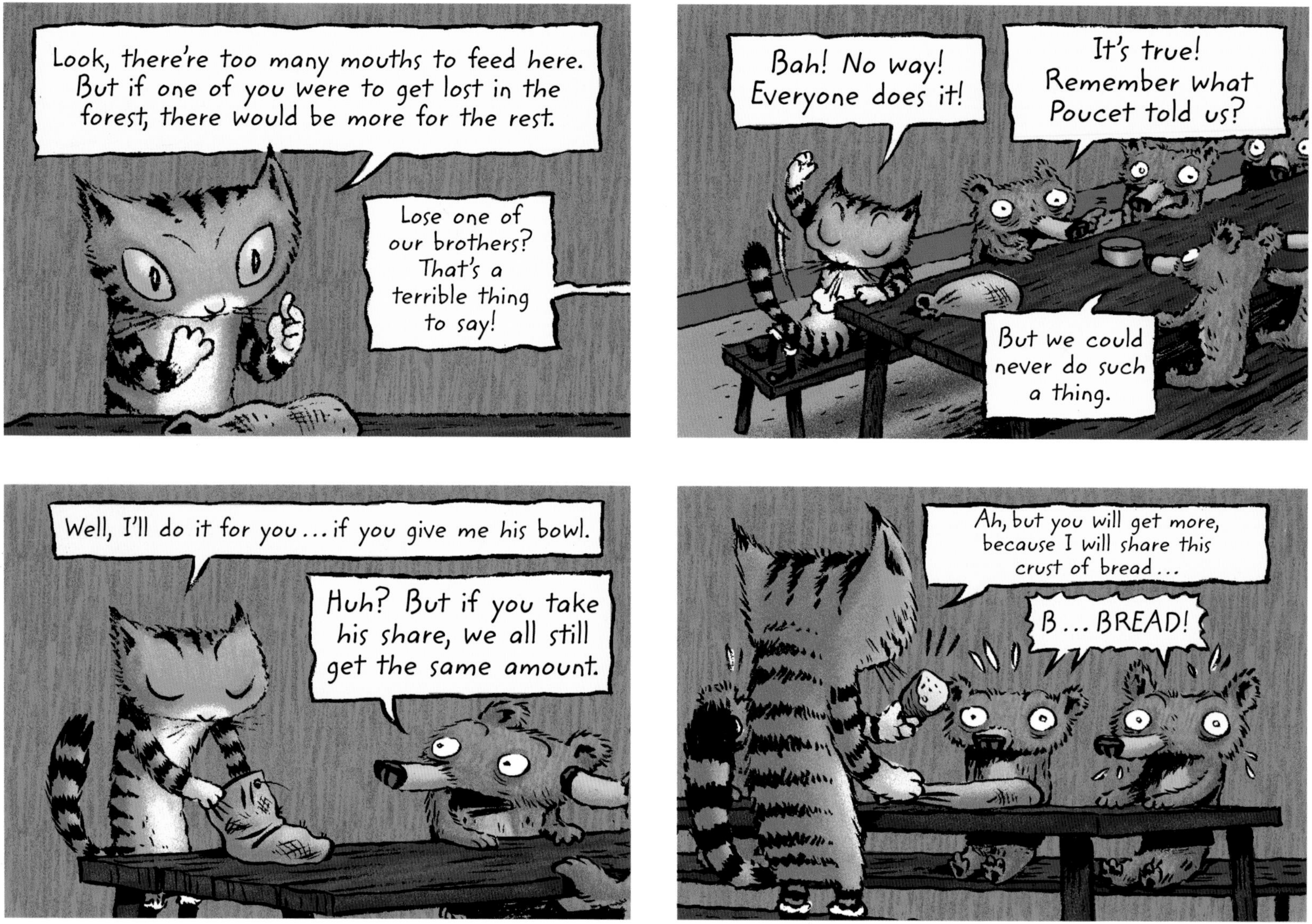
Look, there're too many mouths to feed here. But if one of you were to get lost in the forest, there would be more for the rest.
Lose one of our brothers? That's a terrible thing to say!
Bah! No way! Everyone does it!
It's true! Remember what Poucet told us?
But we could never do such a thing.
Well, I'll do it for you... if you give me his bowl.
Huh? But if you take his share, we all still get the same amount.
Ah, but you will get more, because I will share this crust of bread...
B... BREAD!

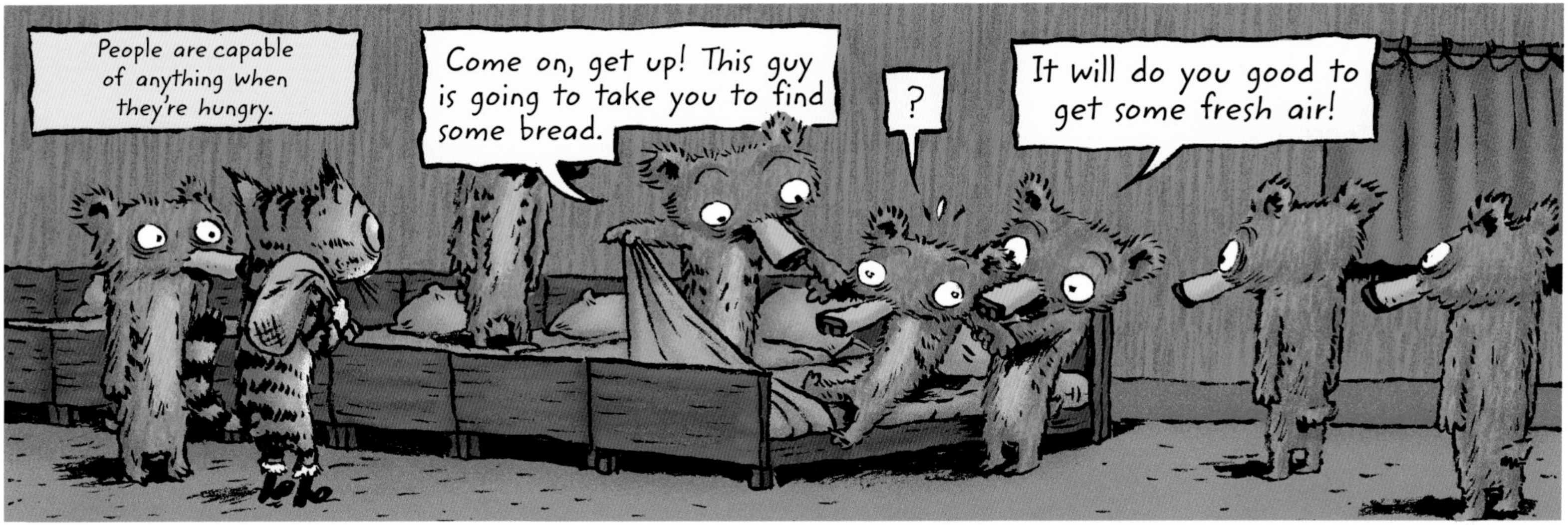
People are capable of anything when they're hungry.
Come on, get up! This guy is going to take you to find some bread.
?
It will do you good to get some fresh air!

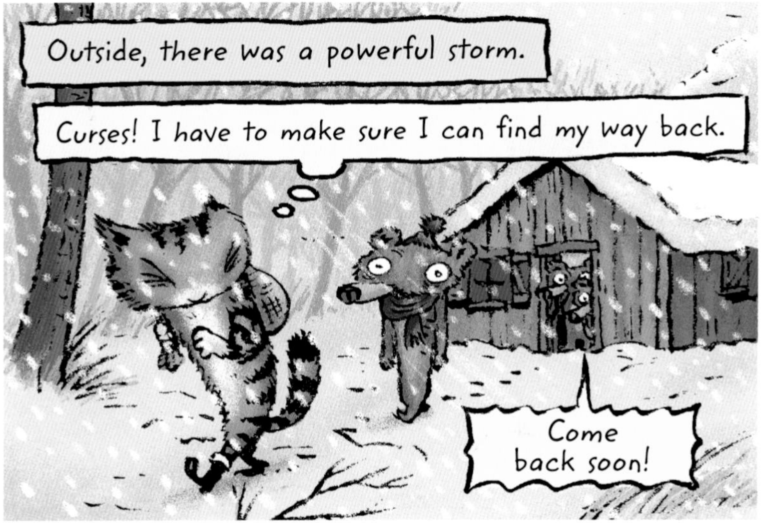
Outside, there was a powerful storm.
Curses! I have to make sure I can find my way back.
Come back soon!

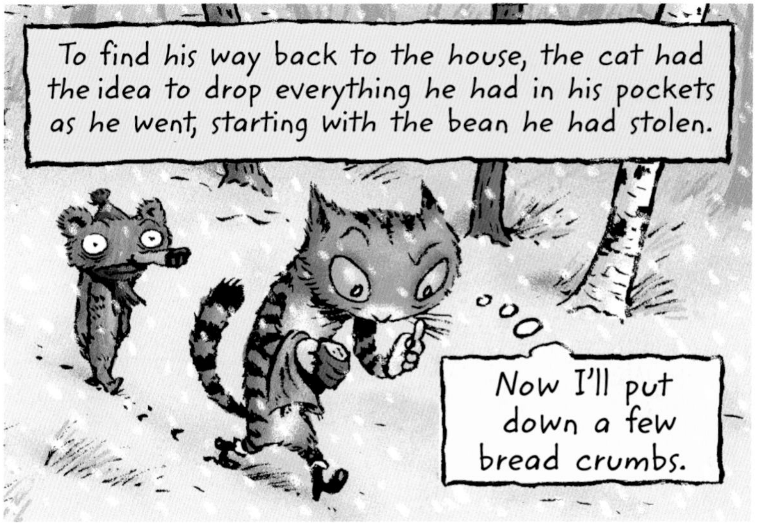
To find his way back to the house, the cat had the idea to drop everything he had in his pockets as he went, starting with the bean he had stolen.
Now I'll put down a few bread crumbs.

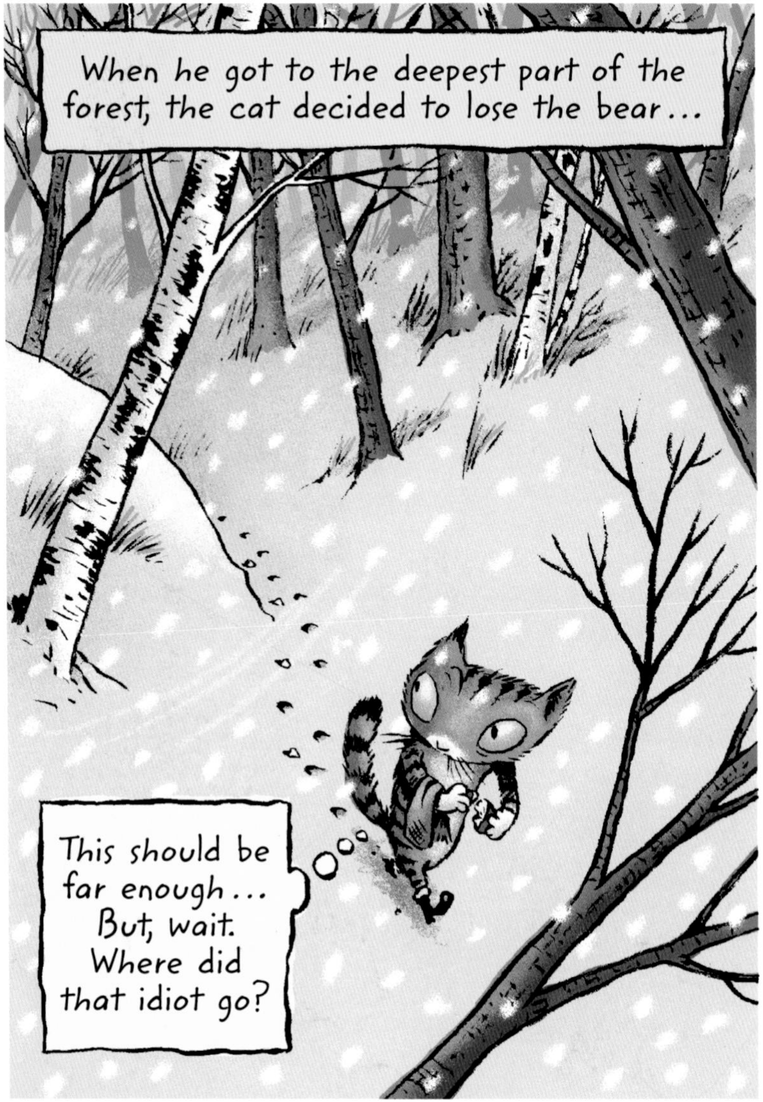
When he got to the deepest part of the forest, the cat decided to lose the bear...
This should be far enough... But, wait. Where did that idiot go?

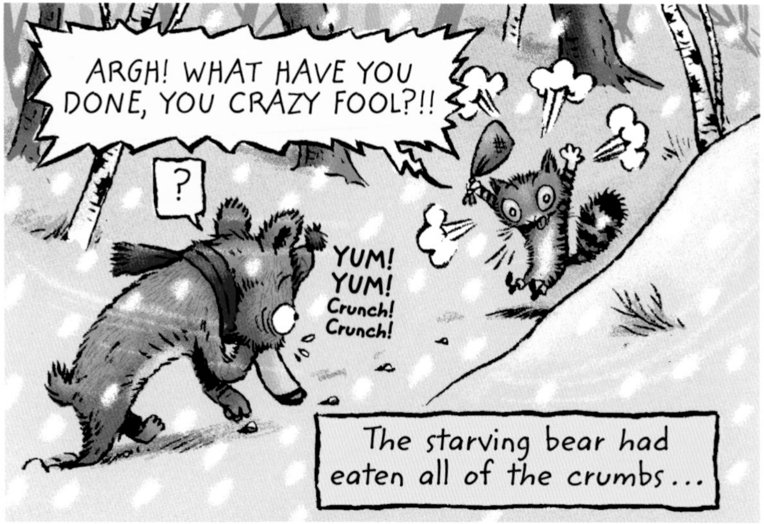
ARGH! WHAT HAVE YOU DONE, YOU CRAZY FOOL?!!
?
YUM! YUM! Crunch! Crunch!
The starving bear had eaten all of the crumbs...

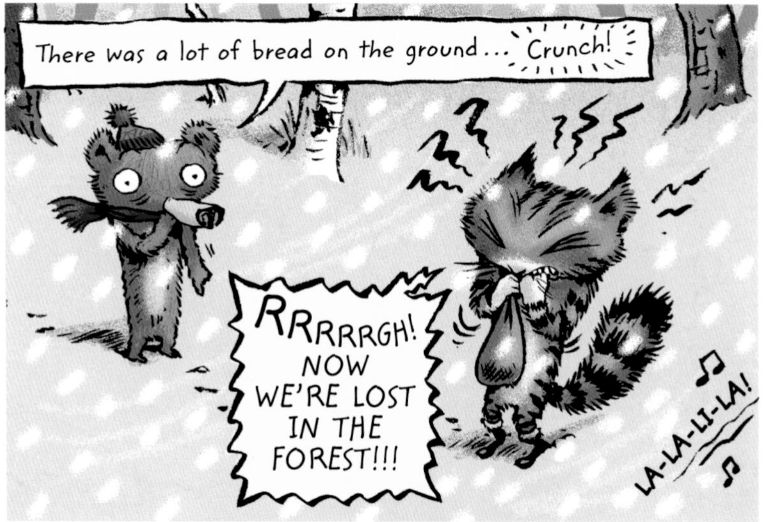
There was a lot of bread on the ground... Crunch!
RRRRRGH! NOW WE'RE LOST IN THE FOREST!!!
LA-LA-LI-LA!

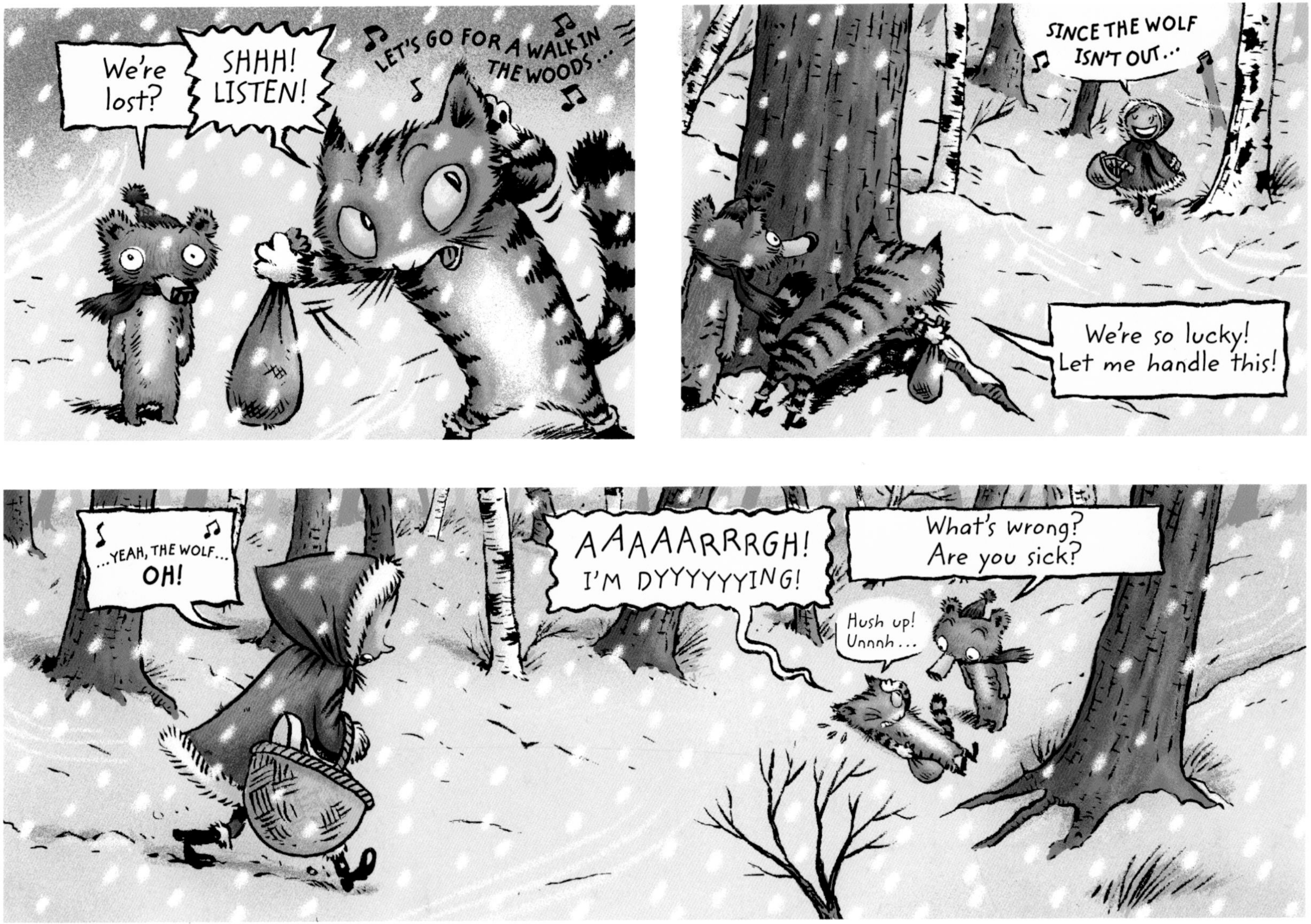
We're lost?
SHHH! LISTEN!
LET'S GO FOR A WALK IN THE WOODS...
SINCE THE WOLF ISN'T OUT...
We're so lucky! Let me handle this!
...YEAH, THE WOLF... OH!
AAAAARRRGH! I'M DYYYYYYING!
What's wrong? Are you sick?
Hush up! Unnnh...

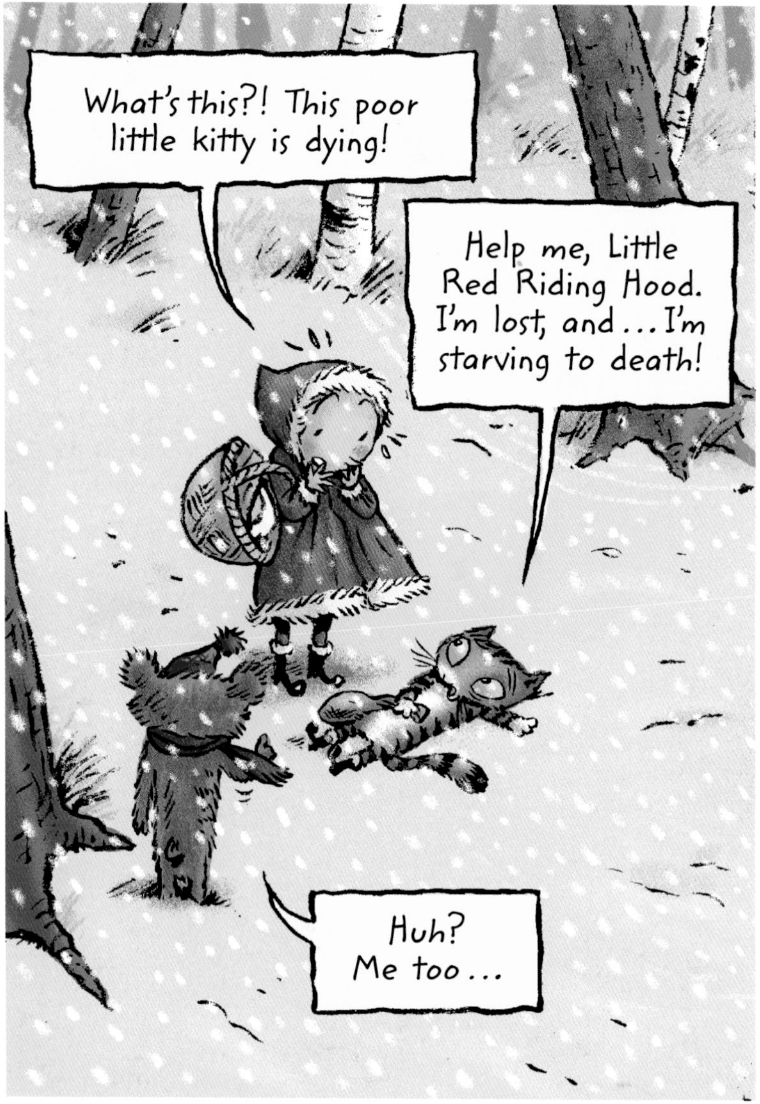
What's this?! This poor little kitty is dying!
Help me, Little Red Riding Hood. I'm lost, and . . . I'm starving to death!
Huh? Me too . . .

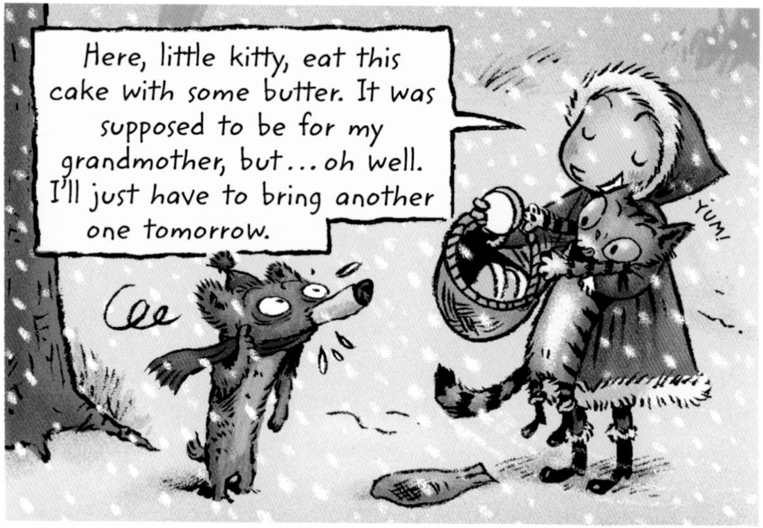
Here, little kitty, eat this cake with some butter. It was supposed to be for my grandmother, but . . . oh well. I'll just have to bring another one tomorrow.
YUM!

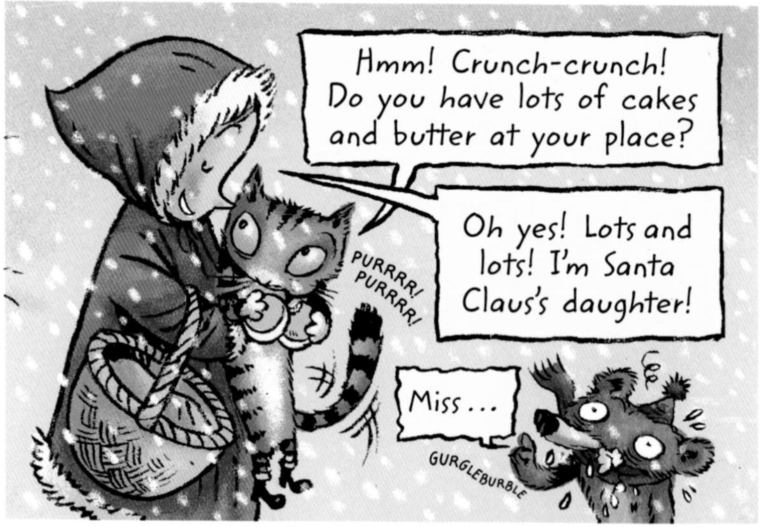
Hmm! Crunch-crunch! Do you have lots of cakes and butter at your place?
Oh yes! Lots and lots! I'm Santa Claus's daughter!
PURRRR! PURRRR!
Miss . . .
GURGLEBURBLE

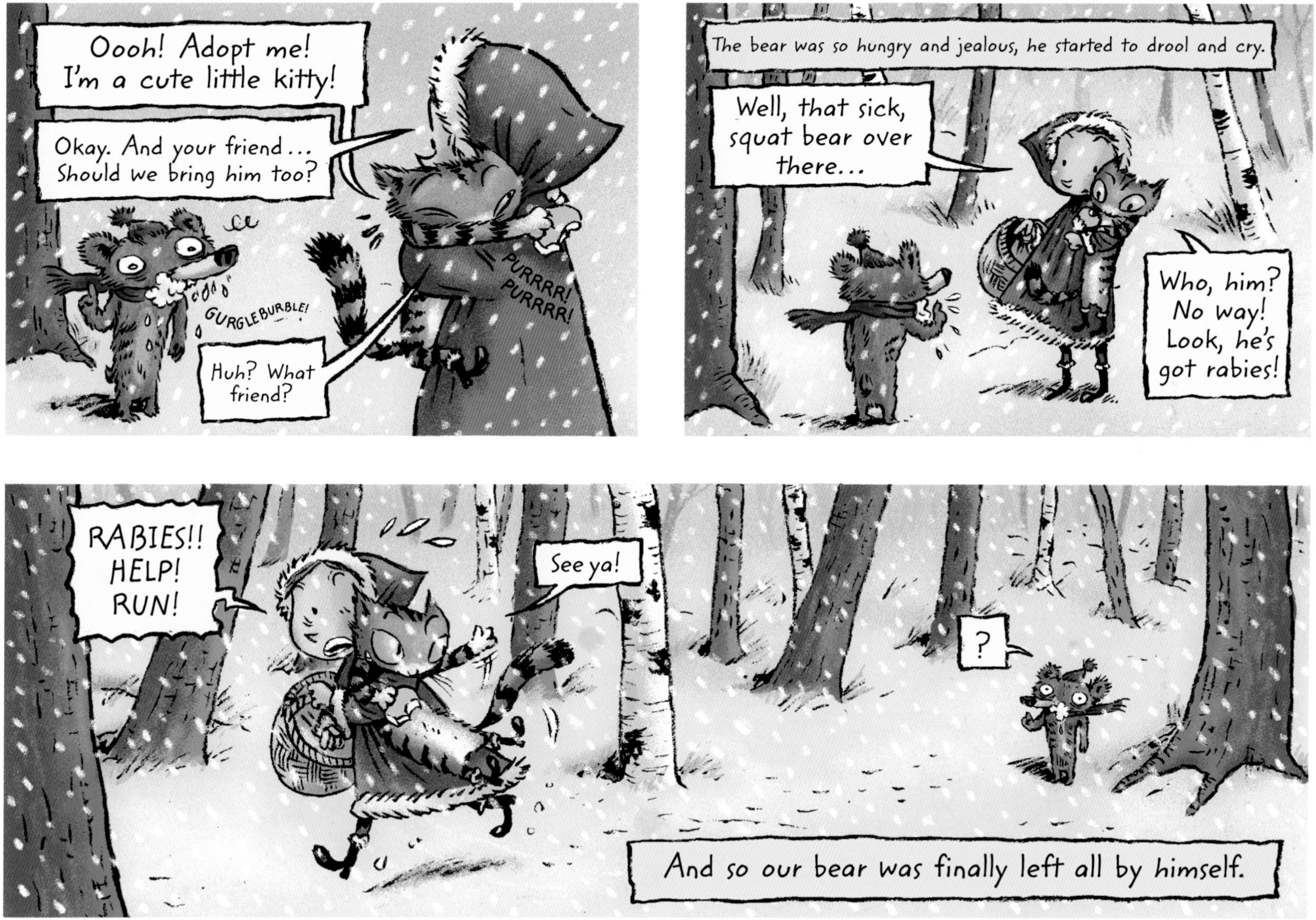
Oooh! Adopt me! I'm a cute little kitty!
Okay. And your friend... Should we bring him too?
Huh? What friend?
GURGLEBURBLE!
PURRRR! PURRRR!
The bear was so hungry and jealous, he started to drool and cry.
Well, that sick, squat bear over there...
Who, him? No way! Look, he's got rabies!
RABIES!! HELP! RUN!
See ya!
?
And so our bear was finally left all by himself.

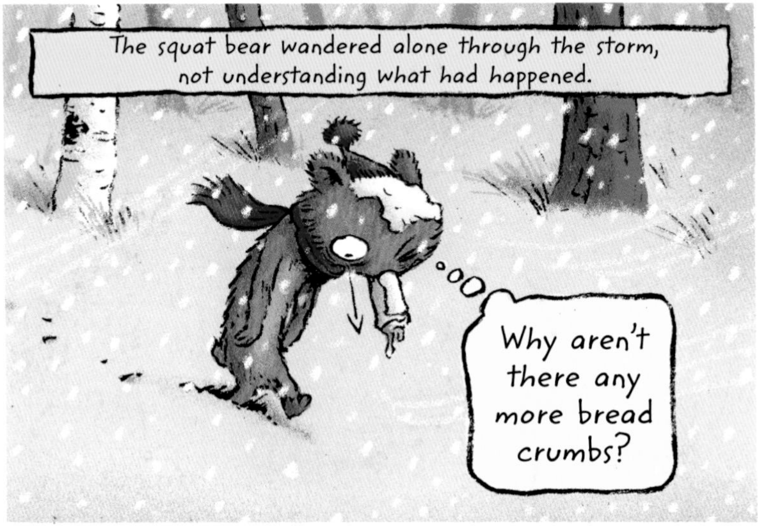
The squat bear wandered alone through the storm, not understanding what had happened.
Why aren't there any more bread crumbs?

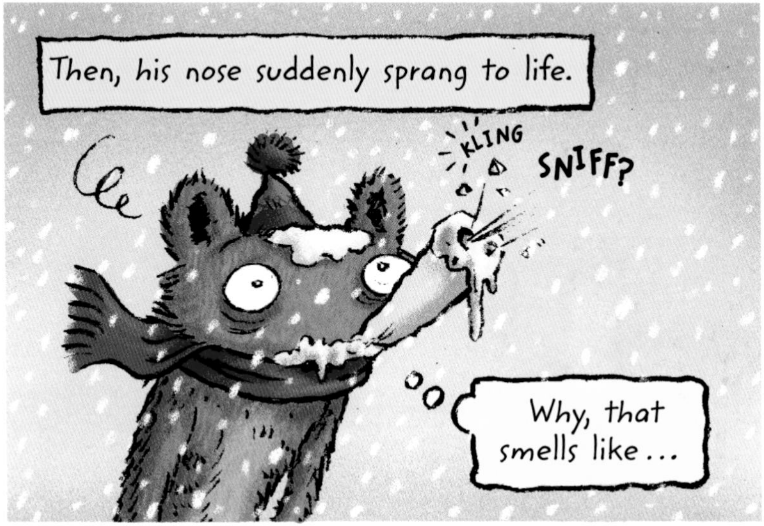
Then, his nose suddenly sprang to life.
KLING
SNIFF?
Why, that smells like...

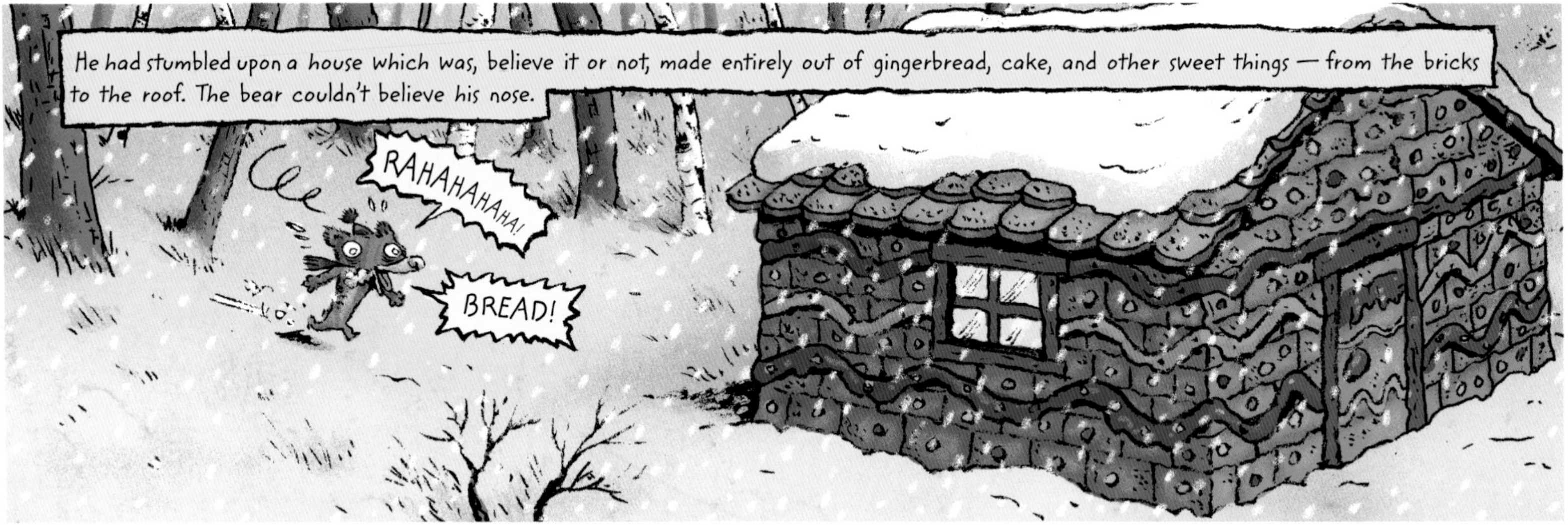
He had stumbled upon a house which was, believe it or not, made entirely out of gingerbread, cake, and other sweet things — from the bricks to the roof. The bear couldn't believe his nose.
RAHAHAHAHAHA!
BREAD!

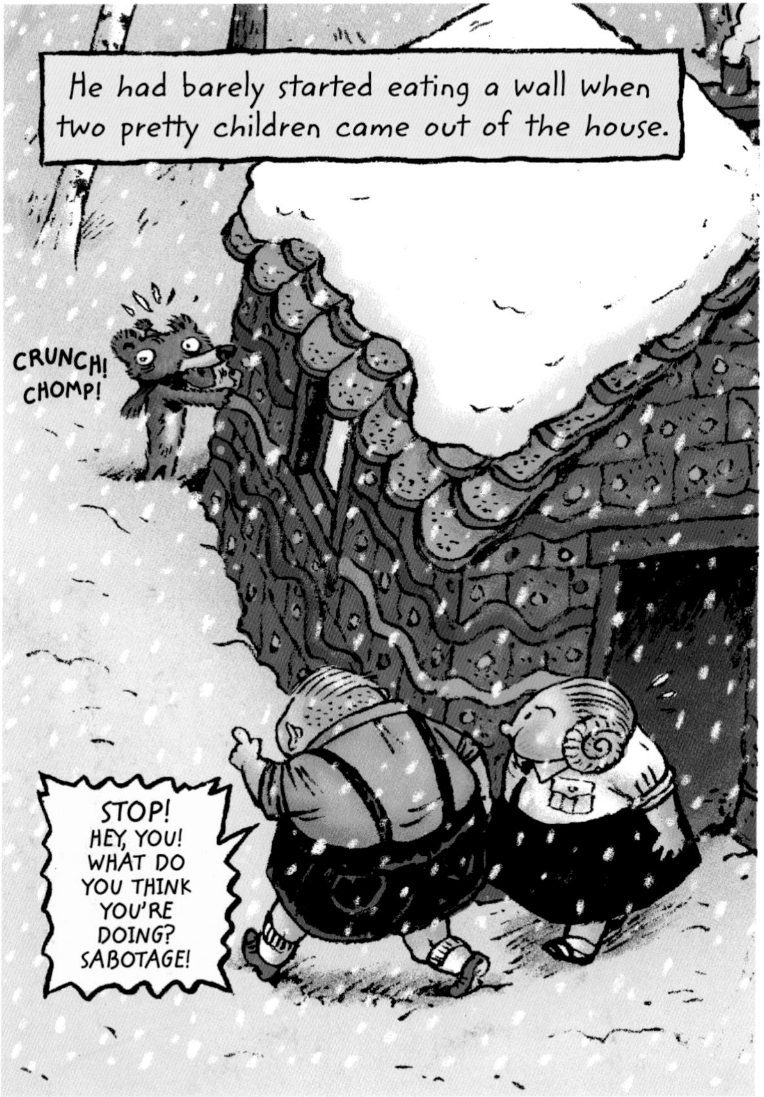
He had barely started eating a wall when two pretty children came out of the house.
CRUNCH! CHOMP!
STOP! HEY, YOU! WHAT DO YOU THINK YOU'RE DOING? SABOTAGE!

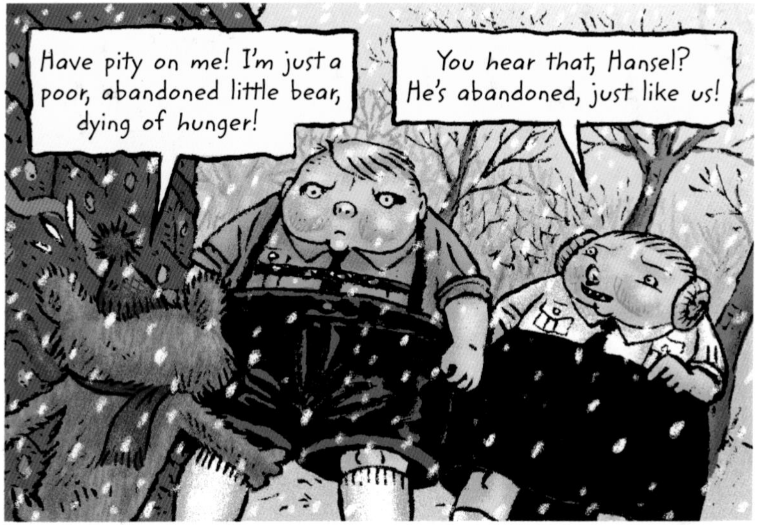
Have pity on me! I'm just a poor, abandoned little bear, dying of hunger!
You hear that, Hansel? He's abandoned, just like us!

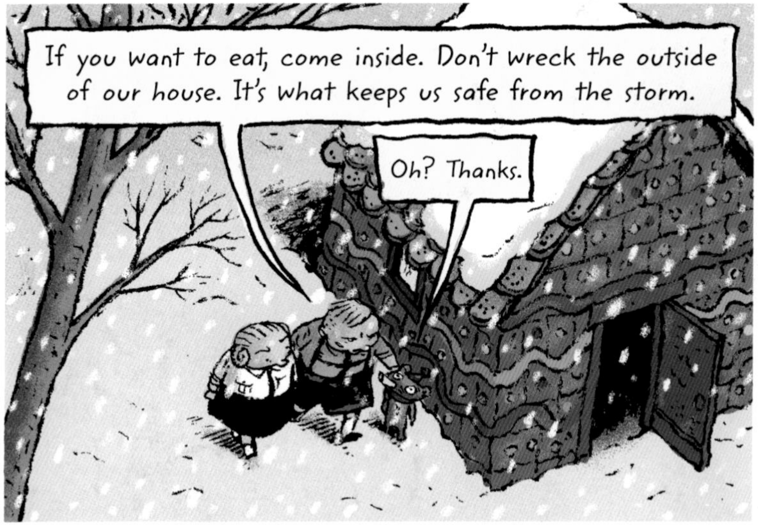
If you want to eat, come inside. Don't wreck the outside of our house. It's what keeps us safe from the storm.
Oh? Thanks.

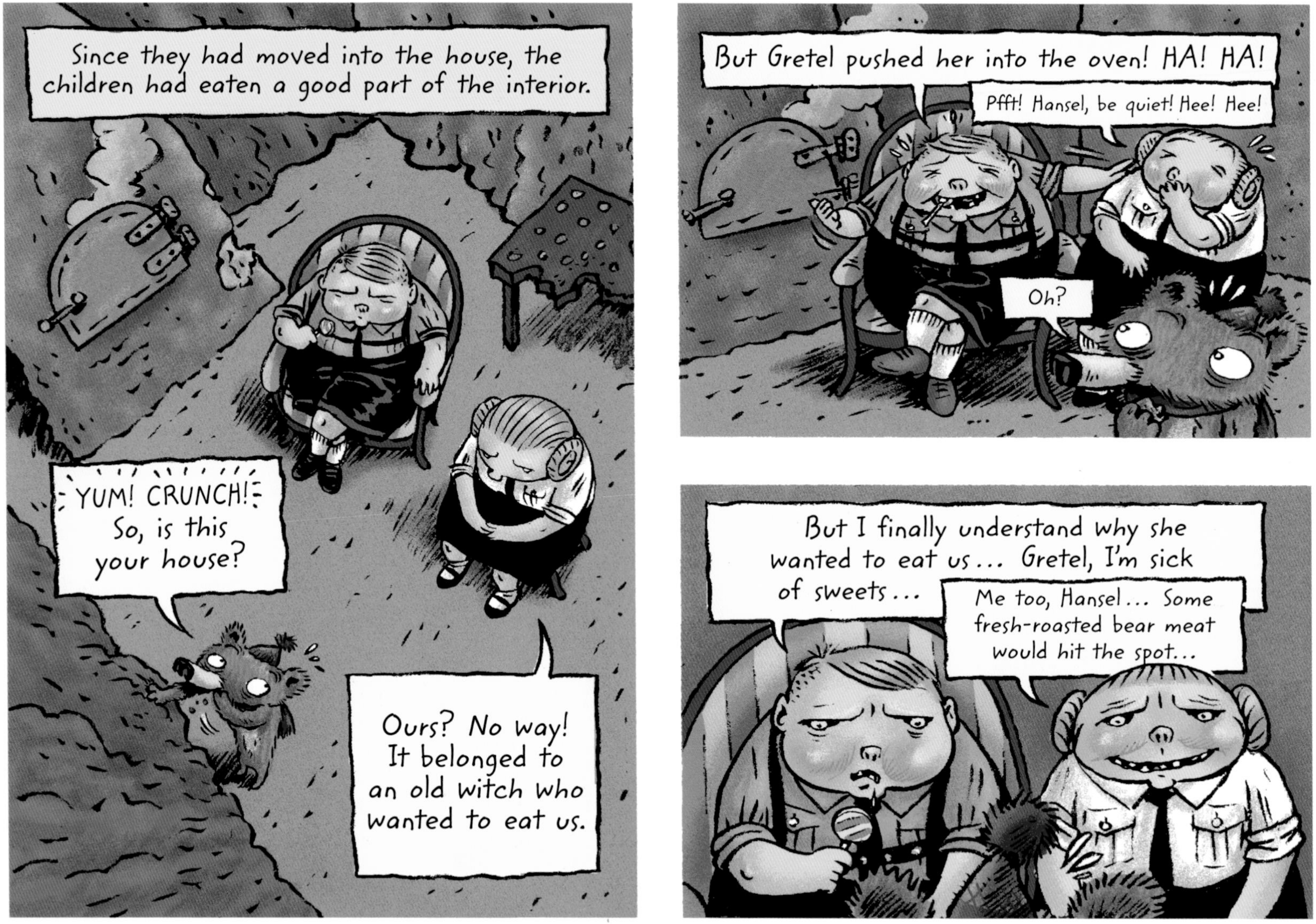
Since they had moved into the house, the children had eaten a good part of the interior.
YUM! CRUNCH! So, is this your house?
Ours? No way! It belonged to an old witch who wanted to eat us.
But Gretel pushed her into the oven! HA! HA!
Pfft! Hansel, be quiet! Hee! Hee!
Oh?
But I finally understand why she wanted to eat us… Gretel, I'm sick of sweets…
Me too, Hansel… Some fresh-roasted bear meat would hit the spot…

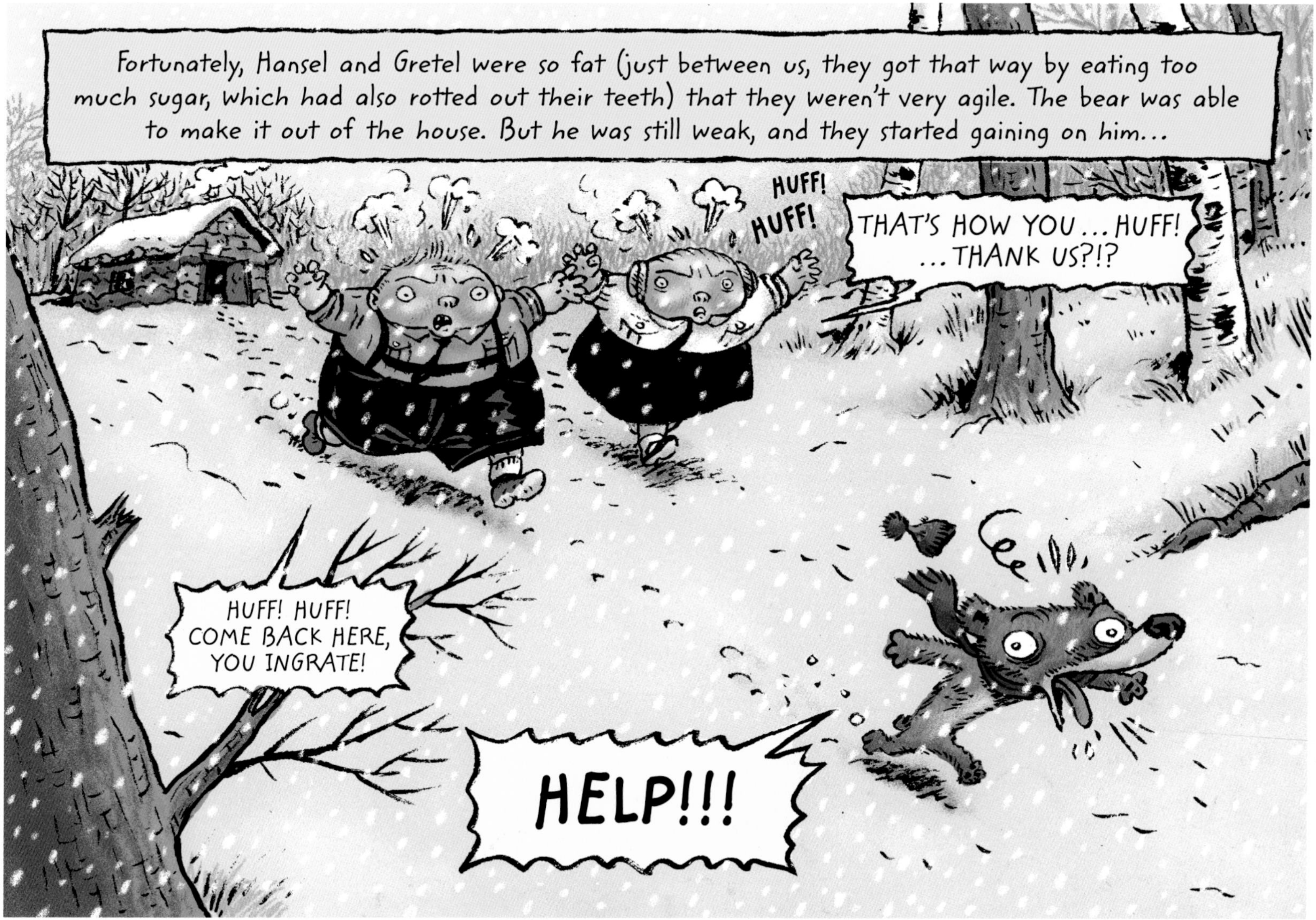
Fortunately, Hansel and Gretel were so fat (just between us, they got that way by eating too much sugar, which had also rotted out their teeth) that they weren't very agile. The bear was able to make it out of the house. But he was still weak, and they started gaining on him...
HUFF! HUFF!
THAT'S HOW YOU ... HUFF! ... THANK US?!?
HUFF! HUFF! COME BACK HERE, YOU INGRATE!
HELP!!!

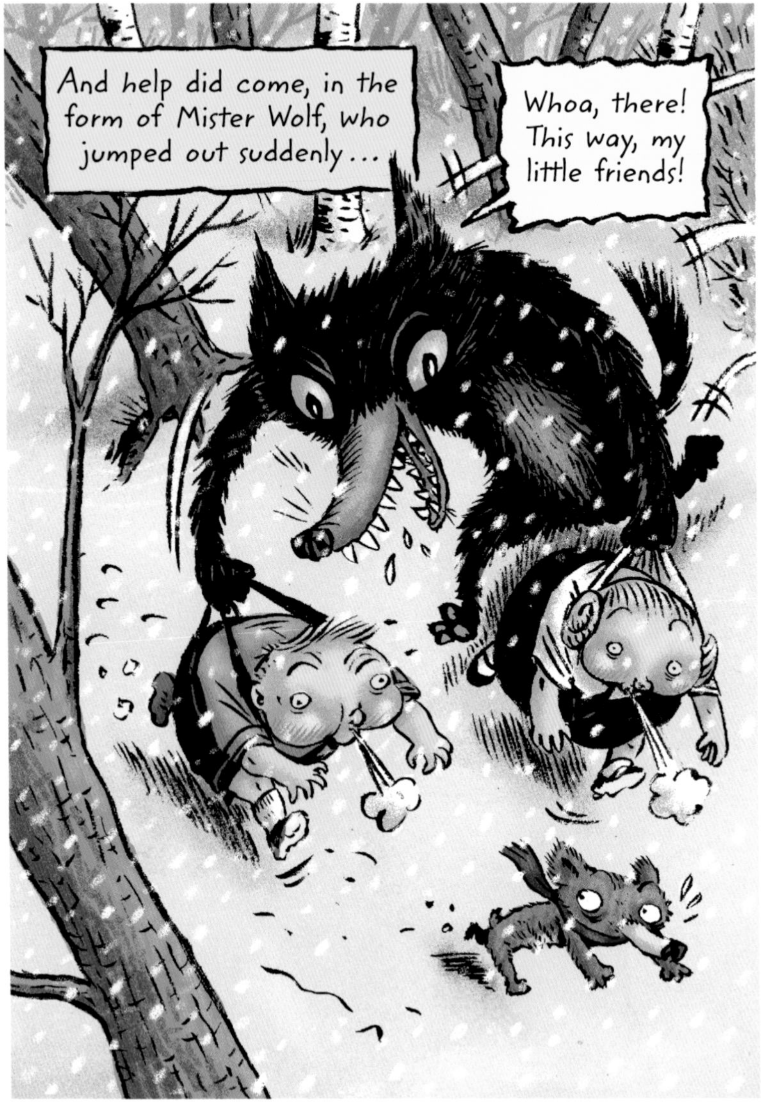
And help did come, in the form of Mister Wolf, who jumped out suddenly...
Whoa, there! This way, my little friends!

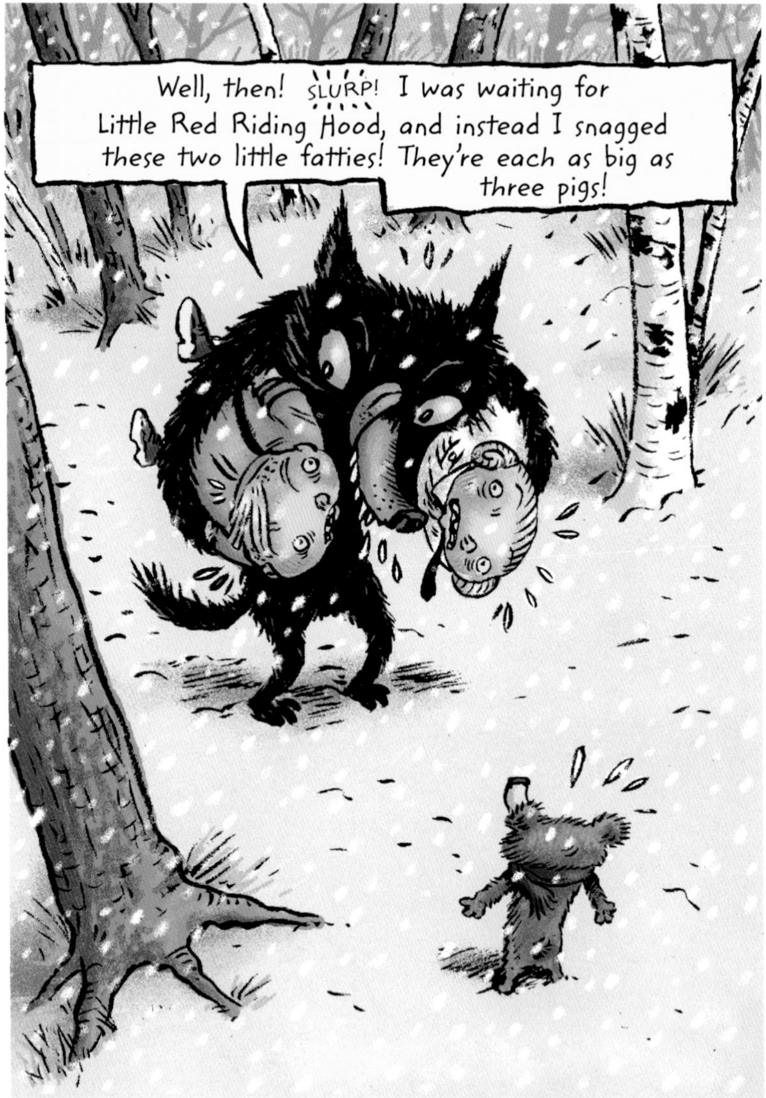
Well, then! SLURP! I was waiting for Little Red Riding Hood, and instead I snagged these two little fatties! They're each as big as three pigs!

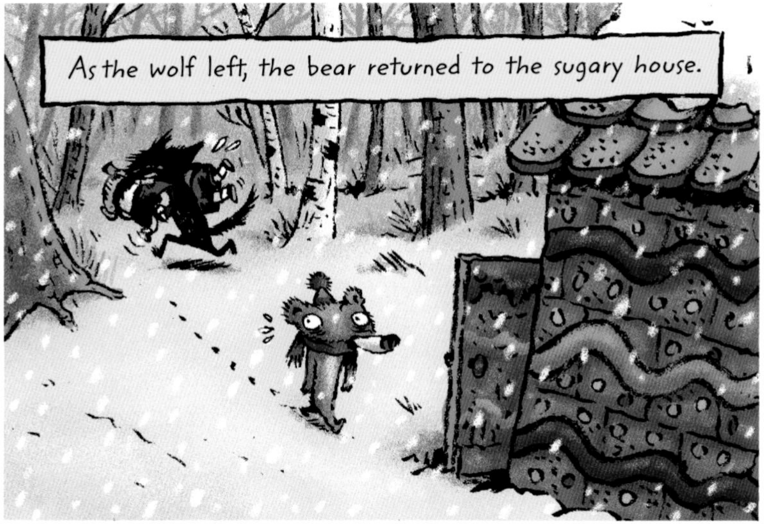
As the wolf left, the bear returned to the sugary house.

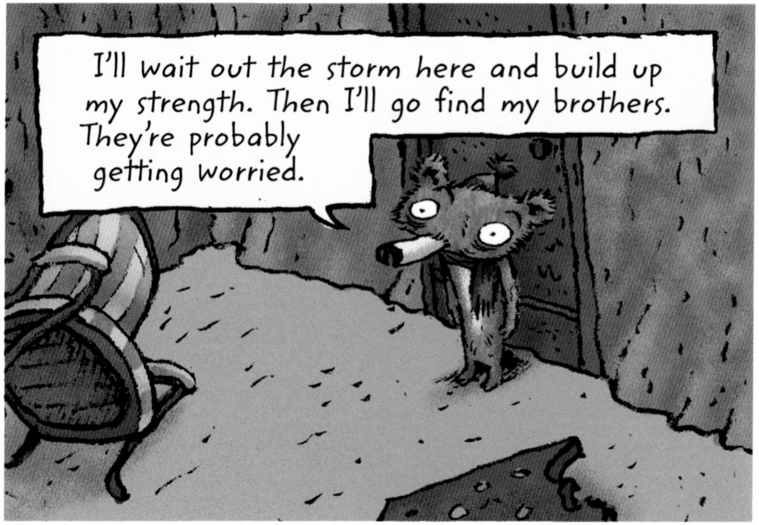
I'll wait out the storm here and build up my strength. Then I'll go find my brothers. They're probably getting worried.

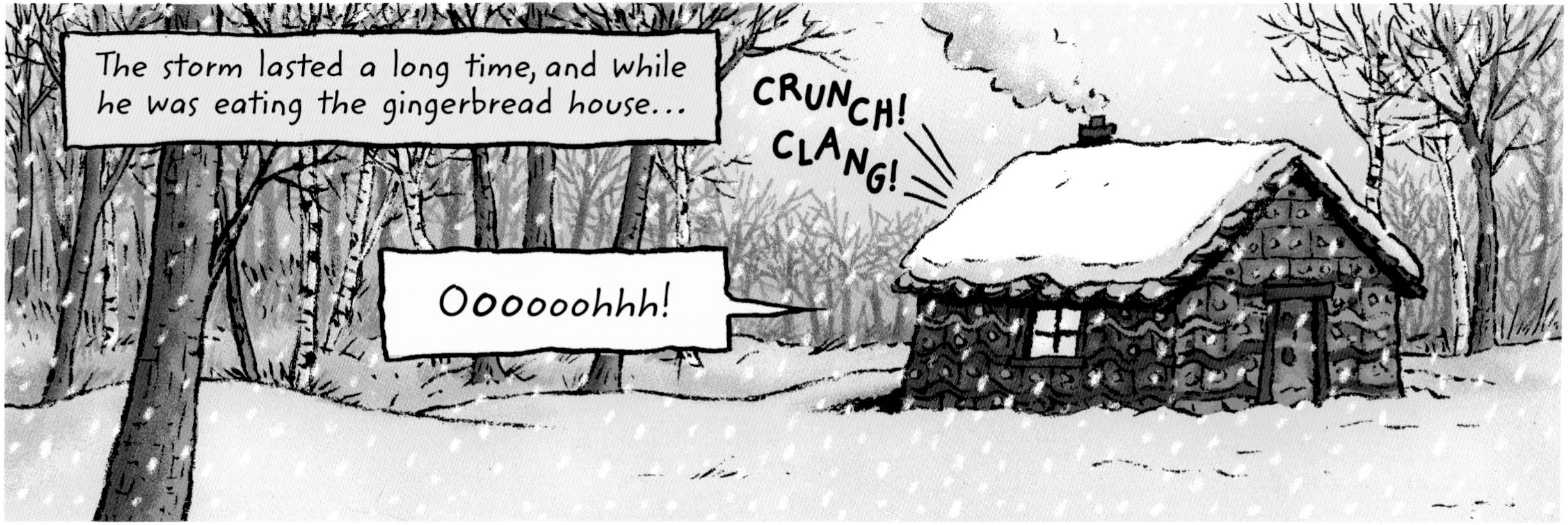
The storm lasted a long time, and while he was eating the gingerbread house...
CRUNCH!
CLANG!
Oooooohhh!

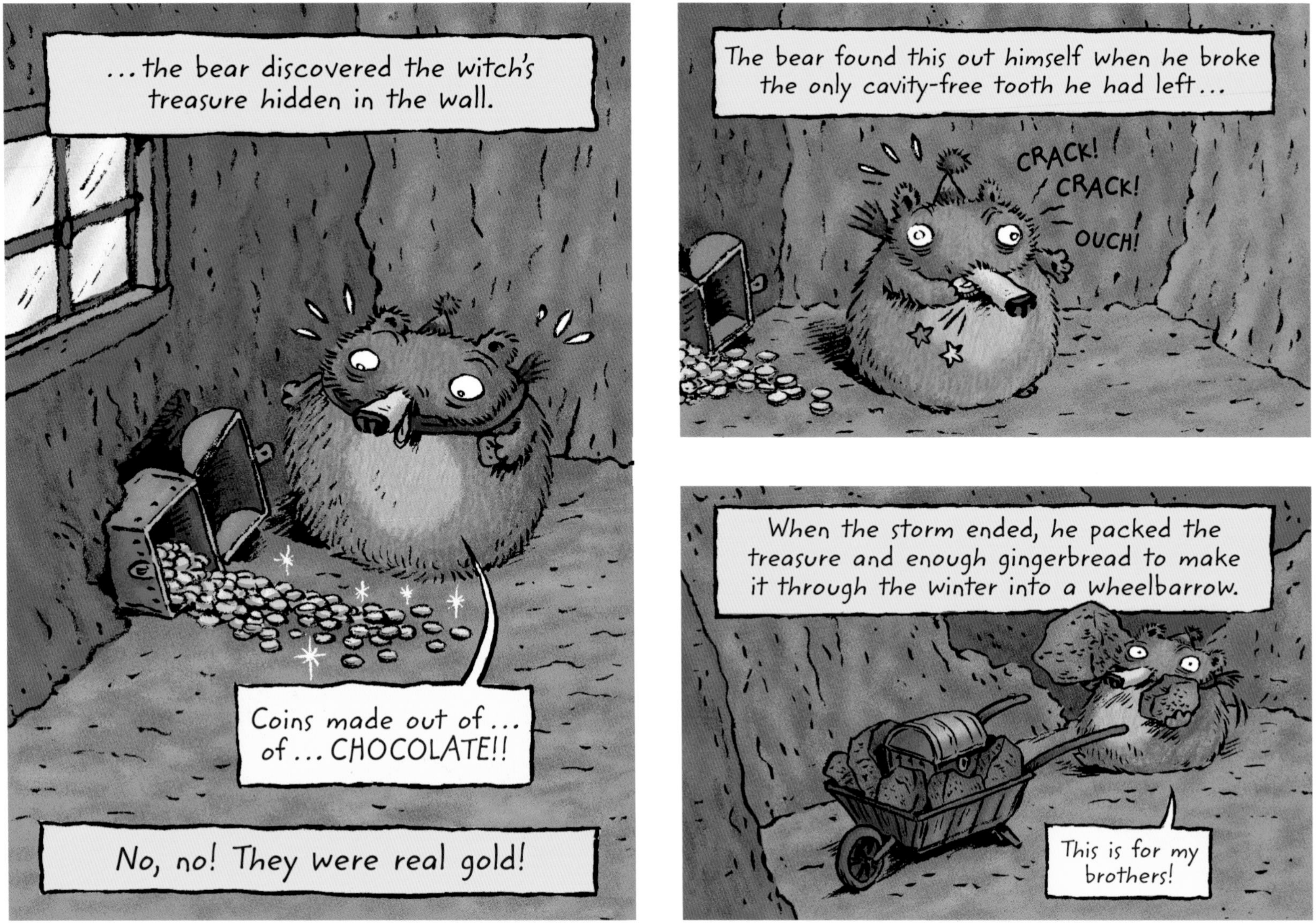
...the bear discovered the witch's treasure hidden in the wall.
Coins made out of... of... CHOCOLATE!!
No, no! They were real gold!
The bear found this out himself when he broke the only cavity-free tooth he had left...
CRACK!
CRACK!
OUCH!
When the storm ended, he packed the treasure and enough gingerbread to make it through the winter into a wheelbarrow.
This is for my brothers!

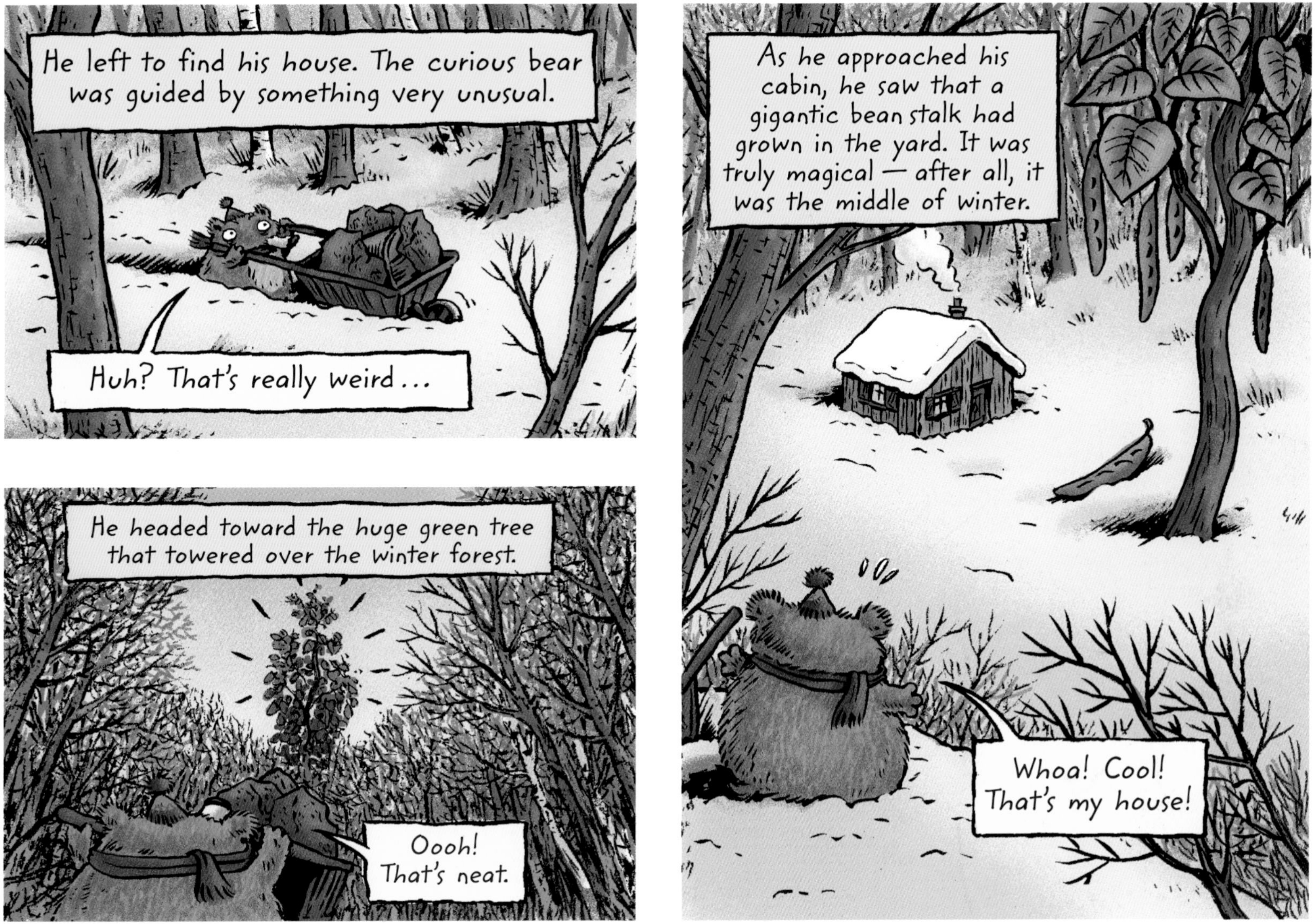
He left to find his house. The curious bear was guided by something very unusual.
Huh? That's really weird...
He headed toward the huge green tree that towered over the winter forest.
Oooh! That's neat.
As he approached his cabin, he saw that a gigantic bean stalk had grown in the yard. It was truly magical — after all, it was the middle of winter.
Whoa! Cool! That's my house!

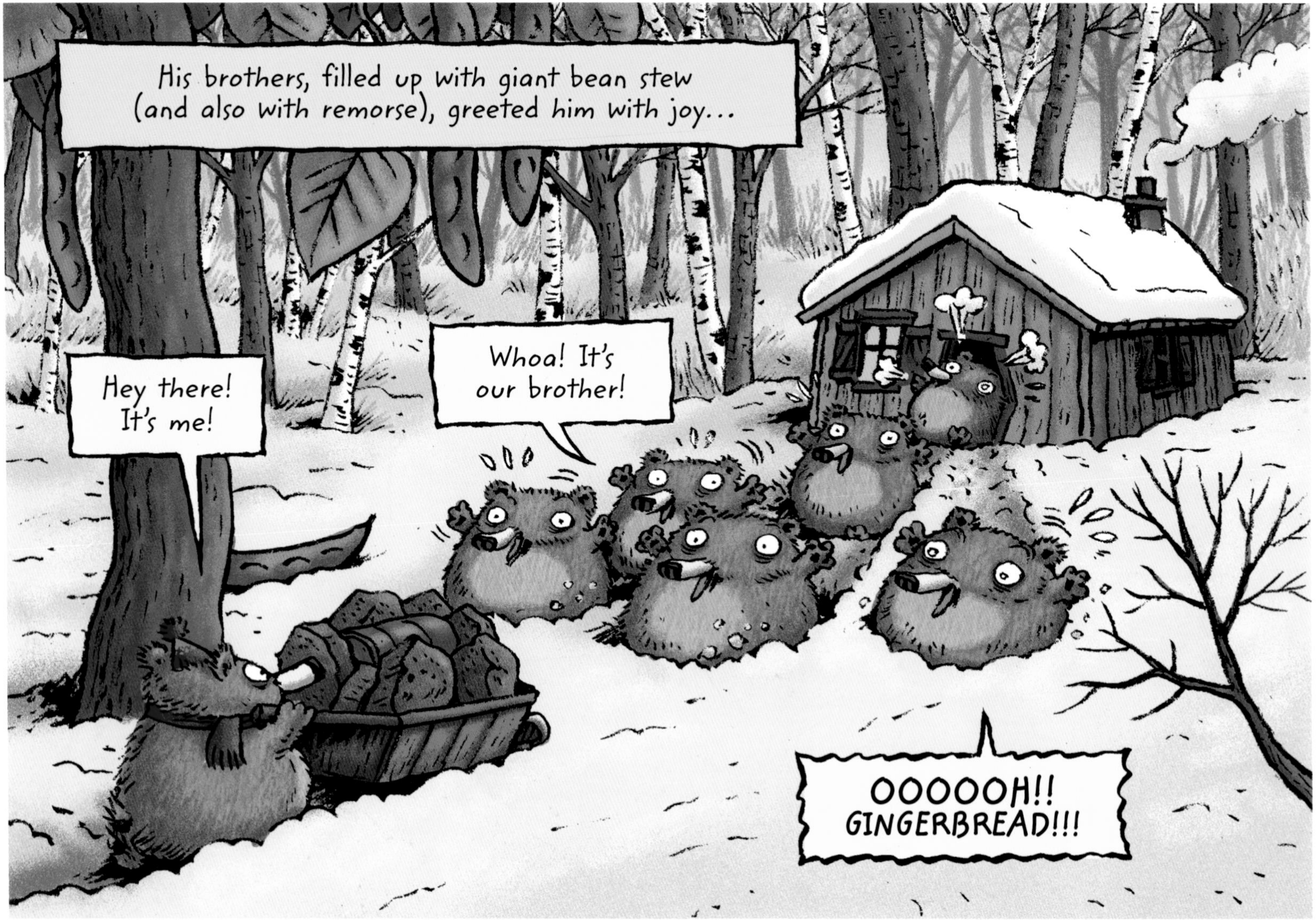
His brothers, filled up with giant bean stew
(and also with remorse), greeted him with joy...
Hey there! It's me!
Whoa! It's our brother!
OOOOOH!! GINGERBREAD!!!!

They had a little party to celebrate their reunion. The formerly lost bear ate a delicious bean soup, and the rest ate all of the gingerbread.

Hey! Tomorrow we can use the treasure to buy some butter and some gingerbread bricks!

CHOMP!
CHOMP!

Once they had eaten everything, the stuffed bears went to bed.

SNOOOOOORE!   SNOOOOOORRRE!

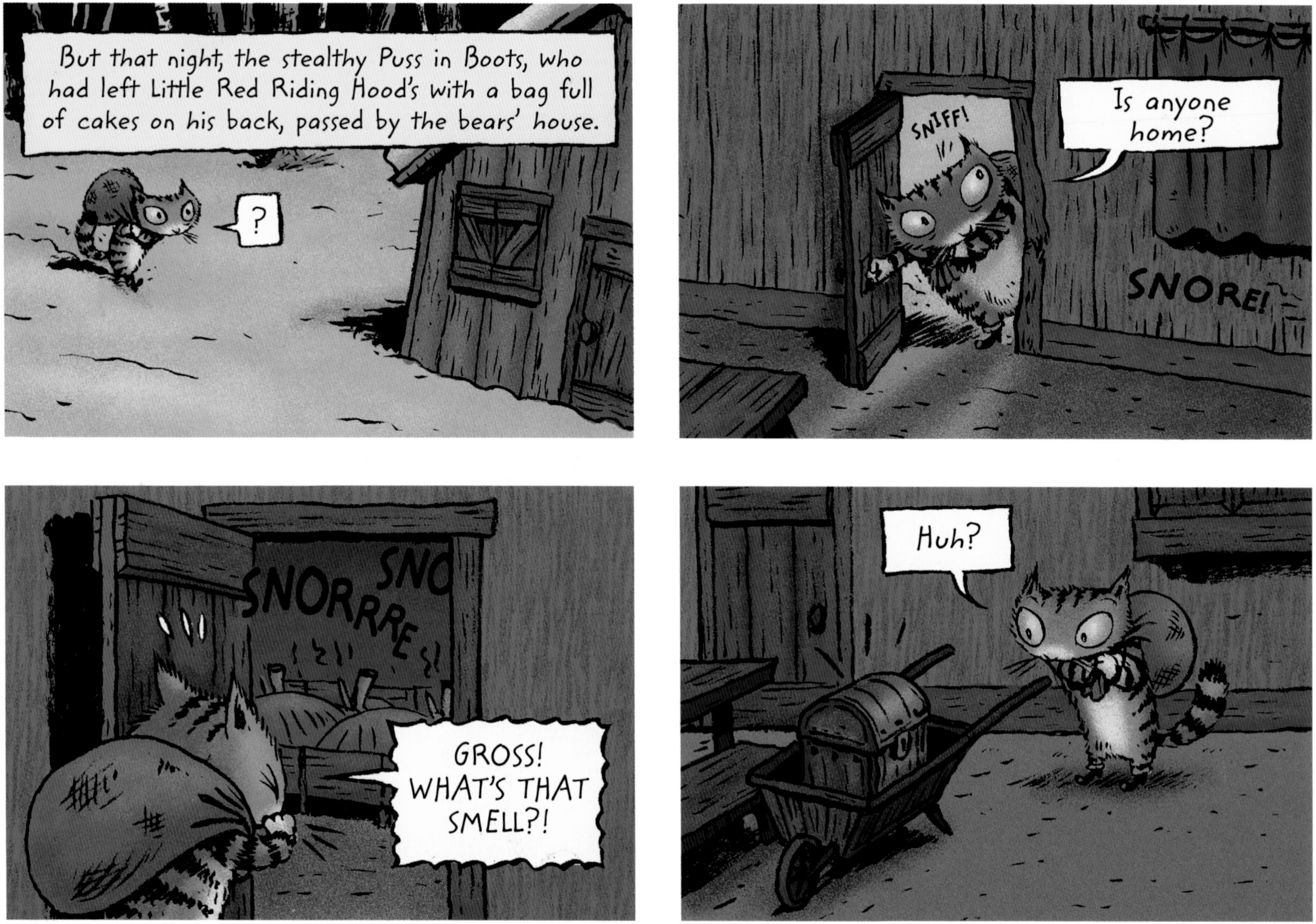

But that night, the stealthy Puss in Boots, who had left Little Red Riding Hood's with a bag full of cakes on his back, passed by the bears' house.
?
SNIFF!
Is anyone home?
SNORE!
SNORRRRE
SNO
GROSS! WHAT'S THAT SMELL?!
Huh?

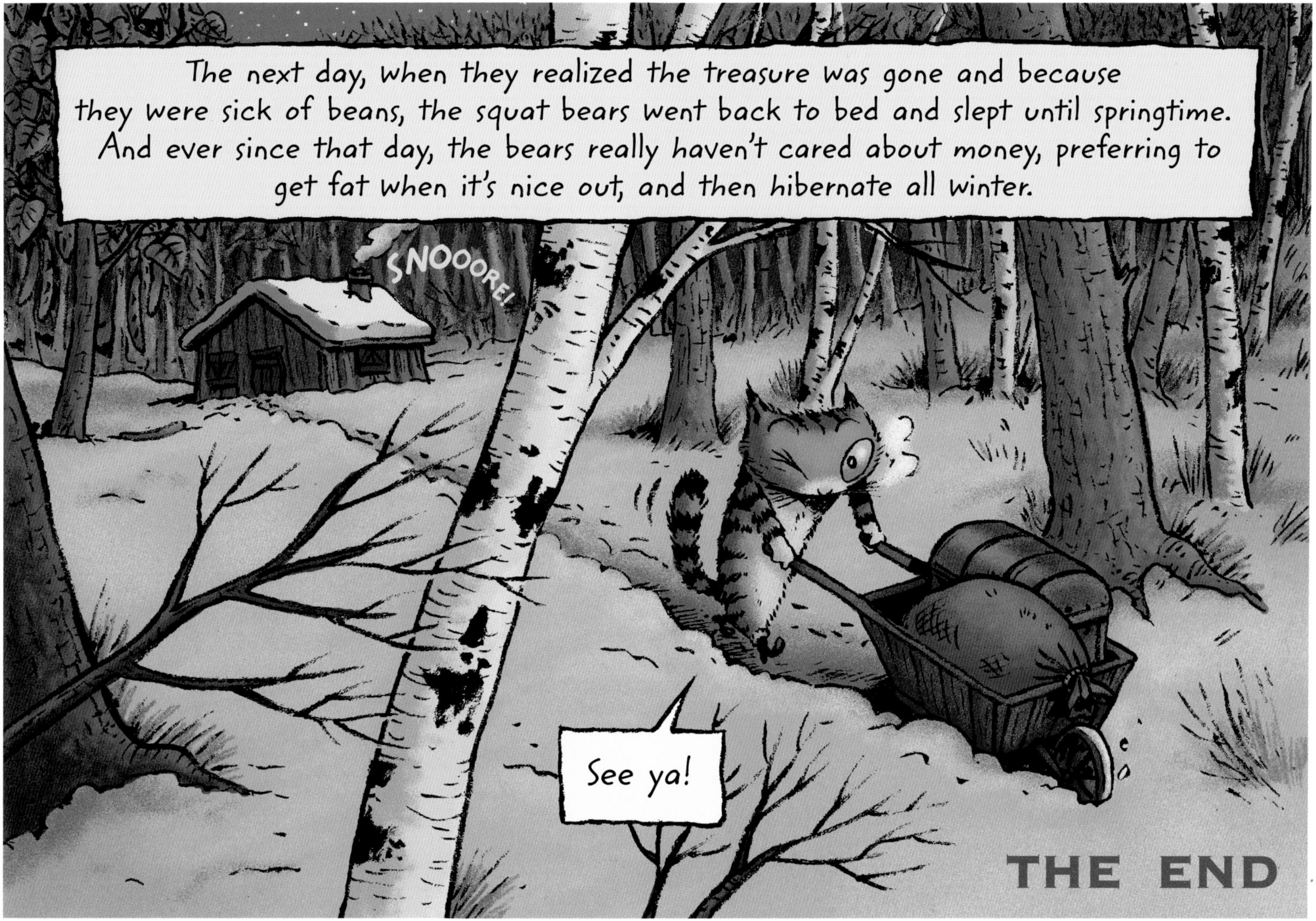
The next day, when they realized the treasure was gone and because they were sick of beans, the squat bears went back to bed and slept until springtime. And ever since that day, the bears really haven't cared about money, preferring to get fat when it's nice out, and then hibernate all winter.
SNOOORE!
See ya!
THE END

THE HUNGER OF THE SEVEN SQUAT BEARS
ÉMILE BRAVO

Translation: J. Gustave McBride

First published in France under the title: *La faim des sept ours nains*
© Editions du Seuil, 2005

English translation © 2011 by Hachette Book Group, Inc.

Yen Press
Hachette Book Group
237 Park Avenue, New York, NY 10017

www.HachetteBookGroup.com
www.YenPress.com

Yen Press is an imprint of Hachette Book Group, Inc.
The Yen Press name and logo are trademarks of
Hachette Book Group, Inc.

First Yen Press Edition: February 2011

ISBN: 978-0-316-08361-4

Library of Congress Control Number: 2010928572

10 9 8 7 6 5 4 3 2 1

RRD/SCP

Printed in China